The Placebo Effect

For my parents Sita and Rama Rao Banagiri,
for watching over me from the other realm

The Placebo Effect

I Think, Therefore It Exists

VANAJA BANAGIRI

PARTRIDGE
A Penguin Random House Company

ISBN: Hardcover   978-1-4828-3771-1
           Softcover   978-1-4828-3770-4
           eBook   978-1-4828-3769-8

To order additional copies of this book, contact
Partridge India
000 800 10062 62
orders.india@partridgepublishing.com

www.partridgepublishing.com/india

Gratitude

I will forever be indebted to the following forces without whose involvement this book would have remained just another manuscript:-

Mother divine, for inspiration.

Penguin Random House, for believing in me.

Mona Ramavat, a journalist and promising writer, whose recently discovered flair for editing adds to her artistry of words. Thank you Mona, for smoothening the edges.

I will forever be indebted to the stars in my universe without whose influence my life would be mere existence:-

Damodar Parthasarathy, for being the wind beneath my wings.

Aniruddh Sameer & Pauleen, for unconditional love, acceptance and presence.

Kartik, Kripa, Varun & Shaila, for unlimited love, energy and laughter.

Uma Panchal, for being there no matter what.

Maya & Shankar, for standing by me and encouraging me to bash on regardless.

Anjli Paul, for reinforcing my faith in altruistic friendships.

Nalini Gangadharan, for supporting me in all my endeavours.

The Prophecy

Vishwamitra:

Don't desert me, my special one,
Without you, my soul mate,
I would never have known love or hate,
You're my sun, my moon, my dawn.

Here I was, an ascetic, a sage,
Until you decided to come along,
And teach me how to love and long,
Now you say, love is a cage.

You're an embodiment of beauty,
Of life, of passion, of soul,
You're my obsession sole,
Now you say, it was just a duty.

Don't desert me, my beloved,
If you do, will return my rage,
I can no longer be a celibate sage,
After having longed and loved.

Menaka:

It was never meant to be, o sage,
Of penance, of power, of purity,
I happen to be a celestial beauty,
For me, love's a needless bondage.

It is for you, the earthly being,
A mortal, to be captivated,
It is destined, it is fated,
To be ensnared by your craving.

Your body is your cause and its effect,
For you to survive, you need desire,
That will set your soul afire,
Only then you feel, you're perfect.

My passions have a purpose,
And they are fleeting,
Be it parting or meeting,
I have no need to possess.

It is for you to chase and pursue,
The object of your obsession,
You'll be bound by the illusion,
That'll for sure ensue.

Listen ye, as I pronounce, o prefect,
It is in the destiny of your case,
You men and women, to chase,
The lure of sexual effect

– The Placebo Effect.

Prologue

She had finally come face to face with her tormentor! And the revelation left her both stunned and shaken up. For 10 long years, Menaka was haunted by nightmares in which a faceless stranger spoke to her in voices and scared her beyond endurance, always lingering just at the edge of her consciousness. She had visited therapists, gone through hypnosis in vain. On the contrary, they had become more intense, if that was possible. Sometimes, the faceless form warned her of consequences with fatalities that she didn't pay heed to at first. But when they started coming true unfailingly, life turned into an insufferable torturous mess!

The form was hazy as if clothed in mist; akin to a pattern from the glass partition of a steam room. Mostly, she woke up bathed in sweat with her heart thudding in her ear. On braver nights, she tried looking at the face through the haze, but had invariably woken up just as she managed to slip closer to it. And yesterday she had seen who it was. That too in stark day light. It was the sheer disbelief that shocked her into believing! But how could it even be possible? How could it be? She never imagined it would turn out this way. And yet, was she blind that she couldn't have seen this before? *God! How dumb of me to have suffered for so long*, she thought staring at herself in the mirror. Her face looked like she had just been slapped. The true identity of her tormentor was indeed a slap on her face!

It was a month since she had moved to Auroville, in search of her true self that was lost in the melee of life. What a turbulent life she had led so far! From the age of 20 to 40, her relationships had tossed and churned her entire being with an intensity that left her drained of all zest for life. She got through each day like a zombie. Brushing her teeth, having a shower, eating, existing, dealing with relationship conflicts - or their aftermath - and drifting off to sleep wondering if it would be a restful night or if her tormentor would make a special appearance, after which it would be goodbye to sleep. The dreams usually came early in the morning. Every time she woke up with a pounding heart and switched on the bed light, she would see the arms of the time piece at 5 AM. She had figured, after years of these nightmares that they occurred with clockwork precision. Almost as if her tormentor had set the time aside for a rendezvous with her. She had lucid memories of the first time. Right through her growing up years, Menaka's parents and brother had made fun of how she could sleep anywhere, anytime without any disturbance. She had even slept through mild earthquake tremors once while in her teens. But that seemed like another lifetime. At 30, married for a decade, she had settled, or so she thought, into a secure life. But what she didn't know is that people who don't follow conventions rarely, if they ever do, experience security. And she, for one, had zero regard for anything people said or did. She didn't much care for her own family or friends' opinions when making a decision.

Her first encounter with the tormentor had started off on a night that was no different. Rishi hadn't yet returned home from work. She had had dinner after getting back home and dozed off in the living room sofa. She woke up when she heard the bell ring and opened the door expecting to see Rishi's apologetic face. Instead, she saw a hazy cloaked form who brushed past her and walked in. She tried stopping it but before she knew, it had settled on the sofa. She moved closer gingerly, but not too close. Man, woman, what was this thing? It was hazy, with a humanoid outline with no clear face or form. A ghost? The idea chilled her insides. She asked with as much courage as her numbed mind could muster, "Who are you? What do you want?" It laughed, a soft muffled mocking laughter, and replied, "Have you forgotten me? Strange! Anyway, I have come here to tell you something about Rishi. No, he's not dead but he's as good as dead as far as you're concerned. He can't hear you, see you or feel you. Don't bother wasting your time trying to understand why, when and how. Just go!" Despite her pounding heart, she took a small step closer to see its face. The form lunged at her neck, clutching it hard. "Go away, or I will kill you," and the grip tightened even more till she struggled for breath. She sat up hyperventillating and realized she was still lying down on the sofa. After a few moments of disorientation, her mind told her it was just a dream. She allowed her shoulders to relax slowly. She had slept off without even changing into her nightwear with the watch on her wrist which showed 5 AM. Rishi wasn't back yet and she recalled the dream in a flash. What did it mean and where the hell was Rishi? Just then the bell rang and this time it WAS Rishi, thankfully! When she told him about it, he just brushed it off saying it may have been her worry that he hadn't returned home yet. Sounded logical, so she went with his theory.

The second visit from her tormentor came a month later. She had put the first nightmare behind her after much rumination. Life was back to what it was. Both of them busy with work, he more than her, which was how it had been the last couple of years. That night Rishi and she had dined out after ages. As usual, she kept chatting and he kept nodding mostly and responding to her whenever she repeated a question. The feeling of disconnect hung thick between them. When she asked him if he felt anything had changed between them, he hadn't heard her question the first time. When she repeated it, he had said, "Not at all. Why?" She would probably have offered an explanation had he asked her again. But his question seemed rhetoric to her. They got home, showered, changed, made love and went to sleep. She woke up in the middle of the night feeling thirsty. She had forgotten to keep the jug of water by her bedside, so she walked towards the fridge in the ante-room next to the kitchen. As she picked it up and walked back, she saw the hazy cloaked form standing right in the middle of the living room. She froze. Menaka wanted to scream but lost all awareness of her body, leave alone voice. She braved a look for a clearer glimpse of the face but it was as hazy as before. She stood rooted to the ground as it began to talk. "You still don't recognize me, do you? Never mind, you will, sooner or later. But you know what, you can't ignore me much as you try." She asked in a feeble voice, "What do you want?" The response was the same muffled mocking laughter she had heard the first time followed by, "I want you to leave Rishi. I told you the last time but you didn't take it seriously! If you don't, you know what's going to happen? You're going to die. I am going to kill you." And then the form moved towards her in a flash and roughly palmed her nose and mouth with one hand, clutching the back of her head with another, choking her. Menaka sat up in her bed startled, breathing rapidly. Rishi switched on the bedlight and asked her if she was okay. That's when she realized that the nightmare had returned. She wanted Rishi to hold her close and comfort her but he had gone back to sleep turning to the other side with his back towards her. She looked at the clock. It was 5 AM!

And then there had been a long gap. The third time was on the night she had met Dev at a party. They were introduced to each other by a common friend. When she returned home, unusually Rishi was waiting for her, reading in bed. She had apologized for getting home this late and hit the bed soon after changing. It was already 2 in the morning when she switched off the bed lamp. She drifted off in no time. But soon Menaka woke up to incessant tapping on her right arm. When she opened her eyes, the form was hovering next to her bedside. She sat up with a jolt and looked for Rishi next to her. The bed was empty! And the form said, "You're looking for Rishi? He has gone! Very far away from you! To a place that you don't know or recognize! I told you to leave him but you didn't. Now he has gone! What will you do now, Menaka? That man you met today, Dev; he seems like a stable man. And he's clearly attracted to you. You should go with him. You always wanted to have an easy life, didn't you? In which a man looks after all your needs. Dev will. He's the kind who looks after women. Can't you see? Anyway, now that Rishi has gone very far away from you, do you have a choice? If you don't act quickly, you'll live a life of deprivation. Look at yourself. Look, look," the form taunted, pointing a finger at her body. When she looked at herself, she was shocked. Her clothes were in tatters, exposing one of her breasts, she had bleeding wounds on her arms. She screamed out loud. Somebody was shaking her and she opened her eyes. An alarmed Rishi was asking her, "What happened? Are you okay?" Oh damn! The nightmare had returned. Rishi repeated, "What happened?" She caught herself on the verge of blurting it out. He would just brush it off anyway like he had earlier. Rishi switched on his bed lamp, pouring water from the jug. "Here, drink this." She took a gulp, spilling some and her eyes fell on the clock on his side. It was 5 AM! The coincidence was too strong for her to ignore. She remembered her mom telling her once that early morning dreams came true. But what the hell did her nightmares even mean? The first two had warned her to leave Rishi or die, this one was asking her to go to Dev whom she had met just a few hours ago and why was she wearing torn clothes? Why did she have wounds on her body? She was clueless. Nothing made sense.

It happened again. And again. More repeatedly with greater fear each time. The nightmare would wreck her peace for days with a lingering sense of foreboding. But finally, she had seen the face of her tormentor. Now she recognized who it was, when she was miles away from the place where she had seen them. But even days after they had stopped, she couldn't come to terms with her new found knowledge. Though there was a sense of certainty about her life now. Till recently, her life had been a whirlpool of self doubts. But now she knew whom to turn to and who had the answers to every dilemma... Life is unpredictable but there is one person who knows it all. Menaka had just been given the glimpse of that face. The face that her nightmares were made of!

The Turning Point

He whistled as he walked out of the gate. At last the deed was done. He had liberated a woman from oppression, a battery of people from tyranny and his own self from being a silent spectator. He would remain silent still, come what may, but not a spectator to the drama that would have caused irreversible damage to many lives. He had committed the act. An altruistic one. Life could move on now. For everybody involved. All concerned. To whomsoever it may concern.

Air seemed to shift without movement. The silence of the night deepened a little more. It was a residential area. Purple, yellow flowers were scattered across the empty streets. Just as well. Nothing better than obscurity when all you want is to stay invisible.

Chapter I

"There is no guarantee of what we will get in return for what we give"

Menaka had to leave home and go some place. Home was Hyderabad. Some place happened to be Pondicherry. So here she was at the Chennai airport. She had landed half an hour ago via the Indigo 9 AM flight. An hour and 20 minutes in the air, and an hour before that at Hyderabad airport, an hour-long drive from home to airport. 'Phew, may as well have travelled by train at half the cost!' she thought. But trains in India are anything but comfortable. But then comfort is relative. For that matter, everything in life is, isn't it? What is rich for the poor may not be rich for the elite. What exactly is poor, the rich have no clue! How much wealth is too much? Who knows. Anyway, so here she was at the conveyor belt waiting to collect her baggage. The lady next to her was cradling a baby in her left arm and constantly adjusting the cap on its head with the right. The sultry weather was pretty unsuitable for a cap, even for a baby. But then, what did she know about babies? Or why mothers do what they do? She had never been a mother though she had married twice. In her first marriage, she was neither averse nor keen on becoming a mother. So what was she keen on? Or not? All she knew all her life is that her mind was a hotbed of activity and somehow chewing gum comforted her. It strangely relaxed her, or so she believed. But right now, her mandibles hurt with the compulsive chewing. Just as she moved towards the bin to chuck it, she saw her baggage inching towards her. It was a huge bag, too daunting to drag it off the conveyer and transfer it to the trolley. The lady next to her would be of no help, baby and all. On the contrary, she should be the one offering help. Somehow, with both arms and rather clumsily, she managed to drag it on to the trolley but her shoulder protested as she maneuvered the bag and nearly dropped it on her feet. She started pushing the trolley and her entire right side from the neck to the shoulder felt dead and annoyingly painful. Her shoulders and neck had been vulnerable ever since she could remember. If Rishi was around he would have cracked one of his smart alecky ones, "At least it's not a pain in the ass." She started moving in the direction of the exit arrow. She had been to Chennai a few times in the past but the last time was quite a long while ago. It still looked familiar, though. For that matter, all airports in India looked similar except the dishy ones at Hyderabad and Delhi. The Hyderabad one, she thought, now looked like a hep 20-year-old unlike the *behenji*-turned-mod demeanour it sported a few years ago. Now you could be in Bangkok, Malaysia, Singapore or Hyderabad.

On the way to the exit door, she saw two travel counters one after another, with the sign 'Taxi Service – Mahabalipuram and Pondicherry.' She stopped at the first one, enquired the charges and paid the fare for the airconditioned Indigo. The guy at the counter took the two crisp new 1000 rupee notes from her, opened the drawer below, dropped them in, turned the key, double checked if it was locked and looked up at her. He smiled as he filled in details on a printed receipt with a pen lodged in the receipt book, tore the paper and called out to a boy who was passing by, "Thambi, take madam to Indigo 8666, driver Selva." Thambi rushed to her side, taking charge of her trolley and guided her, "Inda Pakkam (this way) Madam." She walked behind him and realized that she had forgotten to collect the change. Thambi said grinning, "No problem madam. You stay here, I go and bring for you." She liked this Thambi kid instantly. He didn't make her feel like a loser for her absentmindedness. It would have been a different story had she been traveling with Dev. Thambi came running towards her and handed over three soiled 100 rupee notes. "God, these notes are so dirty. I had given him brand new notes," she grumbled. The 20-year-old looking Thambi chuckled amused and told her, a 40 year old woman, "What madam, you're saying? How anybody can guarantee what you get in return for what you give? Dirty or new, value same madam." She was too stunned at his insight to say anything. She spotted the cab with the TN 8666 number plate, a little ahead. She followed Thambi quietly; the soiled notes dampening in her clammy palm. They approached the cab and Thambi patted the boot to alert the driver. The driver stepped out from the front seat and helped Thambi load her huge green samsonite into the boot. "I'm sorry, it's really heavy," she apologized sheepishly. "No problem, madam," responded Selva cheerily, as he slipped in behind the wheel. Thambi just smiled and held the rear door open. She slipped the three soiled 100 rupee notes into his hand as she got into the car. Thambi saluted flashing an excited grin and said, "Thank you madam. Happy journey." She rolled the window down, smiled back and said 'Thank you' too. Dev would have hated both. Generous tip and more so, gratitude towards lesser beings. Selva started the car and stepped on the gas. She leaned back into the seat and closed her eyes, settling down for the three-hour-long drive.

When she opened her eyes, after a brief spell of disorientation, she realized that the car was entering a rather narrow bylane. She looked at the back of the driver's head while enquiring where they were. That's when she realized that in Selva's place was the back of the hood on the hazy form. Just then it turned its face towards her. She should be able to see the features clearly considering she was right behind but no, she couldn't. The same muffled mocking laughter and then the eerie voice, "You don't know where we are? It's so funny. You plan everything, every little move and yet, you don't ever know where you are. Do you at least know, who you are? What do you think you're achieving by running away?" She responded feebly, "I am not running away." The voice growled impatiently, "Just shut up! You're a bloody loser! You're running away because the man you loved has chosen somebody else and the man who loved you is dead! I am the only one you have now and you think you can run away from me?" Even as the voice rose, the car began spinning out of control and came to a sudden halt as it hit a block. She let out a yelp. That's when she heard somebody asking her, "Madam, what happened?" She opened her eyes and realized that her tormentor had no intentions of leaving her alone, regardless of place and time. She regained composure and asked the driver how long it would take for them to get to the destination.

Selva explained that they had almost reached the resort she had booked herself in online. She wondered if she had made the right choice when the car entered a teeny weeny bylane but as the cab entered the gate, she knew instinctively that this was just what she needed. It was a quaint little beach resort with just a few villas. Quiet and peaceful. Her cell phone had run out of battery. Excellent! No phone calls, no text messages! Suddenly, it occurred to her that she had nobody to inform, nobody who expected her call or message. Was that a bad thing? She wasn't sure. All she needed now was respite from her life which had taken on its own course quite out of her control. To add to the mess were the nightmares, coming anywhere anytime these days. She had been to a therapist a few times but nothing had helped. On the contrary, they had acquired a sinister air. Hopefully, this break would put an end to it? What was she going to do after this break? She had no clue what life would be like after she got back from here. She had nobody waiting for her.

The bell boy in uniform collected her baggage while she paid Selva. She followed him to the reception and filled the necessary forms. The receptionist called the duty manager who accompanied her to the cottages. She chose number 18. This number fixation, she had acquired from Dev. But right now, the scenic positioning of the cottage did it rather than the number. Dev had a thing for the number 9. In fact, most people who belonged to affluent families in Hyderabad shelled out big bucks to get a number that totaled to 9, for their cars. The one that got auctioned for huge sums was the 9 series – 0999, 9099, 9990, 9909, 9999. Relatively cheaper were the ones that added up to 9 like 1800, 8100, 6300, 4500, 7200 and such. The reason for 9 being considered auspicious is primarily because any number you add to 9 remains that number. When you multiply 9 with any number, it remains 9. She wondered if the lucky 18 would help her get rid of the nightmares.

She was told to wait for a bit in the coffee shop till the room was ready. She settled down across the window sipping her welcome drink, with a hypnotic view of the seamless ocean. She always found the sea incredibly sexy. Rishi and she had almost died making out on a secluded Goa beach when a giant wave came crashing in. It would have been a perfect death though, while drowning in the waves of pleasure with the one you loved most.

She jumped as a man in uniform informed her that the room was ready. She recovered after a moment and he escorted her to the room where her luggage had already been placed. She tipped the waiter and left a visibly happy man. She plonked herself on the bed looking at the ocean through the French windows. This whole money business bewildered her when she was younger. The world's single biggest obsession, if you ignore sex, cutting across regions and religions was money. Invariably, conversations revolved around money (for men and women) followed by weight (for women, some men) and sex (some women, most men).

Unlike many women, though, her sole obsession was the physical aspect of a man-woman relationship. She could never figure why she pegged everything on this one thing in relationships. Most of her female friends didn't give a damn. Several of them shared how they were relieved on the nights when their men didn't express any inclination. "Oh, I can tell from the way he moves closer and puts his arms around me when he has 'that' on his mind. So predictable that I pretend to be fast asleep at the slightest movement," one of her gym friends had ranted going breathless, thumping on the treadmill. 'That!' To utter the word 'sex' was unthinkable for so many, even in this day and age.

How come she never felt averse to sex? Probably, it had a lot to do with Rishi, who had introduced her to the pleasures. She felt utmost comfort with him and zero inhibitions. Though she couldn't say the same about Dev. Strange that she, for whom it mattered most, had not slept with him before they got married. Not even on the night of their wedding, in fact. "Come on girl," she shrugged and said to herself, "No going back and forth. No comparisons. Live in this moment. For the moment." She had just finished reading Eckhart Tolle's 'Power of now' and she was determined to put it into action. This whole trip by herself, for herself, was the first step in that direction.

Forty eight hours had passed since she had checked into the resort. She had reached here on Tuesday and today was Thursday. All she had done so far was to sit in the balcony and stare at the sea. It was quiet and relaxing. The resort was new and it was not the holiday season. Very few people visited Pondicherry during summers. It was burning but she likes heat compared to cold. She could brave extreme heat. She loves moderate heat. She can tolerate mildly cold temperature. Her bones ache in extreme cold. So what did that make her? Warm blooded or cold? She always thought she belonged to the latter category. Only recently, she had discovered that it was the former, alright. This was just one inconsequential discovery she had stumbled upon which would neither have a debilitating effect nor a positively transformational one. Nevertheless, at least she had embarked on the path of self discovery. It unnerved her to think that at 40, she still had no clue who she was, what she wanted or why she didn't want what she didn't! She thought to herself, "I know I am a woman (pat, pat). I also know I am a vegetarian by upbringing and choice. And a few other such obvious things. What I don't understand is why I never wanted a conventional life? What can be so distasteful about being married to a good man, bearing his children, watching them grow up and enjoying a secure, comfortable life like most Indian women do. But did I stay single, pursue a career passionately, guard my independence and live the life of a non conformist? Nah. Quite the contrary. I got married at 20 to the man I fell in love with (Should that be lust?) to whom I had gifted my virginity – physical and mental. My body loved the experience, my mind (Should that be heart?) felt strangely violated. Somewhat like the soiled currency notes I had exchanged for crisp ones. True, we have no idea what we will end up getting in return for what we give. But then, for the longest time, I was thrilled with what I got in return. Somewhat like Thambi who was thrilled to receive the soiled notes. Is it because I had known that the value is more important. So what happened? When did I change? Where did I lose the plot? That's what I am here to find out. Actually, these are just a few questions I need answers for. The others are:

1. Why did I leave Rishi?
2. Why did I cheat on him knowing well that he loved me? Maybe not in the way I wanted him to, but he did. And I knew that. Yet I left him. Why?
3. Why did I marry Dev even though he was not my type?
4. What is my type? (The two men I married were at the two extreme ends of the spectrum)
5. Why did I want to go back to Rishi after I married Dev?
6. Why did I continue to see Rishi while living with Dev? Why couldn't I just walk out?
7. What am I? Inconsistent or unstable? How did I love one man and live with him for 15 years if I were either?
8. Who am I?
9. Do I seek novelty? If yes, how did I marry the first man I got intimate with and never got intimate with the second man I dumped the first one for?
10. Why did I never have children? (I was young, fertile but never went off the pill)
11. What do I want from life in general? (If somebody asks me what's my idea of the ideal life, I have no answer)
12. What do I want to do from now on? (My life is in a limbo. I have seen two dreadful Ds – Divorce and Death. I have no career. I have zero ambition. My drive is a thing of past. To do this or do that? To

be here or there? Go where from here? I don't even know what this or
that could be here.)

13. What am I seeking? (Am I looking for anything at all?)

Sorry. I know the list seems daunting. But you know what? I haven't listed many
more because I feel crazy in my head even thinking of them. But trust me, if
you know what I have been through, you'll understand me. Though I am not
sure if you can trust me on that one."

Menaka's mind was spinning with the endless stream of conversations she was
having with herself. Before she realized, she had slipped into the memories of
her most recent experience, the chain of events that went back to her past and
all the people who dwell there…

Chapter II

Nainam chindanti shastrani
Nainam dahati Paavakaha
Na chainani kledantyapo
Na shoshyanti maarutaha

Weapons cannot cut the soul,
Nor can fire burn it,
Water cannot drench it,
Nor can wind make it dry.

The death of him who is born is certain,
And the rebirth of who is dead is certain,
It does not, therefore, behove you
To grieve over an inevitable event.

Menaka stared blankly at the priest who was chanting Sanskrit verses from the Bhagavadgita and explaining the meaning in English. His voice wafted in and out of her ears, sometimes audible, sometimes faint. She looked at the sleeping form of the man lying in the middle of the room who refused to wake up. He was still deep in sleep. His face had the most peaceful expression she had ever seen in their life together.

She was wearing a simple white churidar kurta, something which would have made the man who was flesh and blood until a few hours ago, a happy one.

Menaka's hand trembled as she ran it through her hair. 'Needs conditioning,' she thought and felt guilty immediately. For a moment, she paled. Her brother who was sitting on the other side noticed and moved to her side. Her neck hurt and she leaned on him. Her parents had not yet visited. She never really missed her mother but she wondered what had kept her dear father away at a time like this. The first line she spoke since Dev's death was, "Is dad coming?" Prabhat didn't have the heart to tell her that their mother had prevailed over their father to stay away. He lied, "They are in Ooty. Couldn't get through to them. No network I guess." Menaka could tell a lie when she heard one. But she had no energy to probe. She felt as if somebody was sitting on her chest. Like a hand had gone down her throat and churned her insides upside down. Acid played havoc in her empty stomach.

> She sat there wondering if she would ever feel normal enough
> to get up and go out into the world. Like she used to not so
> long ago...

Last evening, as she walked into the compound of her house, there was complete silence as usual. It was a beautiful night. Full moon and stars. A cool breeze would have made it perfect but not a leaf whispered. Something didn't feel right, though. She didn't know what exactly. Some restlessness hung heavy in the air, mingling with the serenity.

As she walked ahead, she saw in the darkness, a figure briskly pacing past her. She couldn't see the face but when his step lagged and he paused for a moment, she felt that she had seen that swagger elsewhere. Pretty closely.

Overpowering silence and the shadows made the moonlight seem ethereal. She approached the door and rang the bell. She heard nothing. No sound of footsteps, no voice of her husband prompting the domestics to rush to the door. Only dead silence. It was almost eerie. She felt a rush of hot air engulfing her for a moment. When she became aware that she'd been simply standing before the main door, she remembered the keys. She rummaged hard and found the sleek bunch in a tiny pouch on the side of her giant sized bag. Just as she inserted the key she heard the sound of running footsteps near the gate. She stopped struggling with the key. Rani, her live in maid, was rushing across. "Where did you go?" Menaka snapped at her, "How many times have I asked you not to leave the house when Saab is alone?"

"I asked Saab and only then left Amma," replied Rani softly, guiltily.

"Oh, so if he's home how come he is not opening the door?"

"Must be sleeping amma. You know how he is."

Yeah. Sure. She knew how he was. Indeed. At least as far as his unearthly eating and sleeping habits were concerned. But that was normal according to him. Rani had taken the keys from her hand and unlocked the door. She pushed it open and it was pitch dark inside. Not a single light was switched on. Now, that was not him. He always had the lights on. Often more than required. Even while he was sleeping.

Sudden panic overcame her and she gripped Rani's shoulders tight. She found she couldn't quite breathe easily. "Don't worry Amma. He must be sleeping upstairs in the bedroom." The underlying fear in Rani's reassurance made her feel worse. Menaka stood rooted as Rani switched on the ground floor lights one after another and went up the stairs turning more switches on as she hurried up.

What would she do without this 4 ft 10 inch woman who held her house together at all times? A sense of marvel for the maid mingled with her discomfort.

Menaka took her time climbing the stairs one at a time. Her mind focused on the rhythm of right foot up and left foot joining it. She would pause and repeat the process. Something was telling her to watch every step. When she was midway she heard Rani shriek. Menaka hurried up asking, "What happened!" Rani was standing at the entrance of the bedroom, the door of which was ajar, pointing inside. Menaka walked in to the bedroom. Dev was sleeping on her side of the bed with his back towards the door. "Arrey, why are you behaving like a mad woman? He's sleeping." She said and walked towards the other side of the bed to wake him up. The side light was on. As her hand touched his shoulder, her eyes fell on his face. And that sight was what her nightmares would be composed of in times to come. His eyes were wide open and lips oddly parted. His face was still. Like it was frozen in time. She shook his body with all the force of a wife in denial, "Wake up, wake up!"

So much had happened in the last five years and yet so little. She felt like she was caught in a time warp. Why had he come into her life, turned it into a tornado, only to disappear into an unending limbo?

Menaka

"I am not a woman. I am a bag full of them. A different woman with a different man. With my dad, I am a demanding brat. He is the recipient of my tantrums, my love, my fussing over, my warmth. I have several endearments for him and can melt his heart with my sobs, happy in the knowledge of the clout I enjoy in the universe of his emotions. Like a key chain I twirl him at my will around my little finger. With my man, I am like a harlot, seeking my pleasure in pleasing him. I am merely his woman; I live for him, winding myself around him. He also bears the brunt of my ire, my vacillating moods, my indifference, my often difficult silence, my conversations... With my friends, I am a gag bag. Trying to entertain them, make them laugh, the whole time. I used to work as a copy writer before in an advertising agency but deep down, I always wanted a life of leisure. That's me, in all forms.

No matter what I did, I was the centre of my dad's globe. And he ruled, pretty much, every region of my life. Especially that which is inhabited by a man. Make that men. In every man I met, got intimate with, I looked for him. In each of them, I found something of him but not all. Not that I treasured every quality of my dad's. I loved some; I couldn't care less about the others. But if you draw a table, 'loved' would far outweigh the 'not-so-loved.' This drawing a table habit of mine has generally got the better of me, landing me in a mess most times. Look at what's going on in my life right now. I left the only man I ever loved and who loved me back, the man I married and stayed with for a decade or more because the table I drew, threw up more –s than +s.

Whenever a relationship troubles me, I draw a table. Depending on the +s and -s, I decide if I want to be in it. Rather, why I should still bother to be in it. In fact, I only draw the table when I'm wondering if I should get out of it. So, on that day, when everything concerning him and me was crumbling around us and the results at the bottom of the table outdid the + ones, I left. Honestly, between you and me, 20 negatives versus 14 positives. Wasn't such a big imbalance, was it? But then, I saw what I wanted to see. Or should I say I didn't see what I didn't want to. I don't know about you, but I have done that all my life. Deciphered, inferred, discarded, accepted whatever suited me at a given point. I don't do it consciously. I don't know if my heart does it or my mind. I don't even know if we command our hearts and brains or they do, us? Anyway, on that day, I didn't like the way he responded with complete apathy towards my existence, so I left. Obviously, I knew where I was headed. So did my car which seemed to travel on auto pilot straight to his house. Little did I know then, you may have seen one, you still have seen nothing. Whatever, I hate clichés. But you get the drift? Yes, there was another 'him'. I had been seeing him for six months. Yes, I did see a lot of my father in him. Did I love him? I guess I did but I was not in love with him. I was always in love with just one man. Nobody is perfect until you fall in love with them. And when you do, they turn sub-human, falling rungs below their original imperfections.

I don't know when I had fallen out of love but I do know that I had begun to find everything about him annoying. In return, he stone walled me. He became distant like there was a screen of glass between us. I could see him and he could see me. I smiled at him and he smiled back. But when I spoke, he couldn't hear me. My words touched the glass and echoed. And when I extended my hand to touch him, all I felt was the icy cold of the glass. During those days when my words were talking to me and he was being untouchable, I met another man at a party. He saw me first, walked up to me and told me I looked like his fantasy. Then he asked me if I would dance with him, I said 'No.' He asked me if he could get a drink for me, I said 'No'. He asked me if I would meet him again, I said 'No'. And soon, I married him. So what happened? I had no clue. I still don't. You know, some of us have no idea what we want or why we do what we do. Clarity has never been my virtue. Or is that a vice? Whatever. I just don't have it in me. So what is it that I have? A vacillating mind with body weight to match, and a heart that overreacts to every just about everything.

I never respond, I only react to people and situations.

Actually, sometimes I think I have a split personality. There are comments and criticisms that I can junk without a blink and there are others I agonize endlessly over. I guess it depends on who it comes from. Society, people, relatives and the likes, I don't care a whit about. Look at the way I have lived my life. I defied my parents at 22 to marry the man I loved. Then I got out of it at 32, again defying my parents. My parents, I tell you, are an amazing lot. First they didn't want me to marry him and then they didn't want me to divorce him. Now you know where I got that see-saw mind from, don't you?

I think I am uninhibited when it comes to expressing love. I can shower my people with gallons of it. With my man, I need to make love to feel close to him. Sex is not an act for me, it is artistry. Then again, I can clam up too if he doesn't reciprocate even once. I can forget all the good times we spent, if he, for some reason, doesn't respond to my overtures. I can be wanton; I can be a prude, depending on the man's mind set. With my first love I was the former, with the second, you'll know. Throughout my second marriage, the thought that came to mind often was to strangle him off once and for all to make sure he doesn't ever abuse those weaker than him.

I have another strong trait. I hate authority. If you ask me to do something, I will not, even if I feel it is right. Or even in my own interest, if you're asserting authority over me. My rebel streak has overstayed its limit and stuck on to me even though it's been two decades past my last teen year. But who cares? This is me. Between my vacillating mind, unconditional rebellion and two radically different men, I think I have made a complete mess of my life. The only saving grace is, I don't have children. If they had turned out like me, even God couldn't have saved them. I wonder if He could have though! Would I have lived any other way? Yes, I think so. On second thoughts, maybe not.

Rishi

I work as an art director in a film production company. But essentially, I am an artist by nature and temperament. And you can imagine what happens to one when he meets his ultimate muse. Menaka was the only woman in the world for me. Don't get me wrong. I have had other women. Many, in fact. But this one nearly finished me with her heat and contempt, passion and lust, the list could go on for a bit. I think a woman can make a man feel like god or a wimp. She made me feel like both intermittently. Every time I felt like god, she turned into a bitch, and the wimp in me crawled out. Just when I was getting used to being a wimp, she switched dramatically into this temptress, and out emerged the god. She used me, abused me, did what she wanted, how she willed and guess what? I let her. One of my friends says that any woman can catch any man if she takes him at the right moment, on the bounce, in the air; going up or coming down. But Menaka didn't try to catch me. She captured me. Mind, body, spirit, will, all there is to me. I still think I should have made an effort to retain her for myself. She was the one for me. She will always be. I tried getting her out of my system by donating her space in my bed to other women but charity has never been my forte. And it boomranged big time and left me feeling guilty and helpless, even. Despite she being the one who'd walked out on me, that too after some serious two-timing.

I have a strength which is also my weakness. Once I set my heart on someone, I don't change. I can't. I have the ability to love everything about them. I loved Menaka's erratic behaviour as much as I loved her knack to make everything seem so good. I loved the way I felt like a stud in bed with her as much as I loved her fiery expletives. She could have used my strength to her benefit, instead she turned it into my weakness. Why, oh why, are women so superficial?

My worst trait I think is my compulsion to treat everything lightly.

For some weird reason, I just must joke about everything, big or small. I can make an art out of trivialising anything. I feel this one characteristic has cost me my dearest relationship. Deep down, I am a seriously intense guy but I don't know why I have no hold over this particular addiction. Talking of addictions, she also hated my smoking. I did give it up for sometime but like she cared. She had already decided to dump me by then. I have a lurking suspicion; she used it as an excuse. Because, when she was into me, she would suffocate me by thrusting her tongue into my throat, even when I smoked a whole pack. That's her. She does what suits her best. Well, almost.

I know, had I tried a bit more, that son-of-a-bitch would never have entered our lives. If only I could eliminate this abominable creature somehow. In my soul, I know this one and hundreds like him may take her body (though I have my doubts if she will ever share it the way she did with me) but her innermost core will always be mine. Minnie, my name for her, will always be mine. Regardless. I know.

Vaidehi

I have always been a conscientious person – a responsible daughter, dutiful wife and a proud mother. I have never been the kind to question norms or push my boundaries to do things my way. I am the kind who is happy to blend in. I have always been a private person and never shared my innermost feelings with even my closest friends. You could say I am an introvert.

I idolized my father and thought Dev was a lot like him when I met him. I have never been a sucker for romance or eternal love. So when I saw a lot of my father in him, I said why not. What I didn't realize was that a father is a father; your mate behaving like your father can spell disaster. I learnt it the hard way, I guess. Anyway, all I ever wanted was a stable marriage and good kids. I also believed in having a serious career. And thank god, for that. If I hadn't pursued one, I would never have been able to get out of the sham that my marriage turned out to be. They say that expectations are the root cause of disappointments. But I never had any. From a man, marriage or life. In fact, I expected to give birth to sons and I wasn't disappointed on that one. My marriage has been my biggest mistake but I am not cynical. I know that all men are not like my husband, now my ex. I thought I could adapt myself to become what he wanted me to be but it just wasn't working for me. My wake-up call came when I stopped recognizing myself in the mirror. Actually, at times when he turned really oppressive, all I wanted to do was to get rid of him, somehow.

I believe that the universe sends messages to me when I need them. Mine came through books. Books have been my life force. My knowledge, support, companionship, everything that matters in life has come from books.

The best gifts of my life are my two sons. I prayed for sons when I was pregnant and I was ecstatic when my prayer was answered twice over. Men, I believe, are the product of their upbringing and surroundings. I, on my part, will ensure that I give my sons the necessary sensitivity and sensibility to be good partners to their future women.

And yeah, I also love my independence. Even though I like blending in than standing out, I'm not fine with the idea of somebody else running my life, attempting to change my life into what they think it should be. I think my marriage has been the best and the worst relationship of my life. Best, because it elevated me to the status of a mother, worst because I almost died trying to fit into somebody's idea of a wife. And no, I am not looking for another man. I am neither into sex nor society.

Dev

I am a hardcore businessman. I have made billions by being ruthless. I believe emotions are a waste of time except where my sons are concerned. And their mother? I don't know really. I married Vaidehi because she looked the decent sort to me. The sort who would understand me and respect my opinions. As it turned out, she did neither. I thought she would be a lot like my mother. My mother's priority had always been my father - though I feel he didn't deserve her respect - followed by us. Initially, I think until my second son was born, Vaidehi seemed content. I don't know how or when her mind started creating trouble. Strangely, we never really fought or argued. She never refused to have sex with me either. Again strangely, I didn't mourn for her in spite of having spent most of my adult life with her.

I was more shocked to realize that I wasn't needed by her. That would still have been okay, if she didn't take my sons away. Them, I miss with all that's me. In fact, I feel life has come to a standstill since I stopped seeing them every day. Thank God for alcohol that has kept my spirit alive. I don't know if I can thank God for meeting Menaka, though. I was at my lowest, when I met her. She looked so lovely, so effervescent, when I saw her the first time. I had never felt this way with any other woman in the first meeting. I didn't expect her to accept me, considering she was always non-chalant, almost indifferent to my expressions of love for her. I was ecstatic when she agreed to marry me and did soon after. But she switched off on day two. She started picking on my weight, my drinking, my behaviour with servants, my socializing, endless issues! God, give me a break! When I said that in her presence, she said she was ready to do that. Give me a permanent break. What does she think? This woman. Does she mean it? Or is it a weapon to keep me on tenterhooks? Anyway, these days even my sons have slithered away to a tiny corner in my mind. The lion's share is occupied by this tigress. Why am I so obsessed with her? She has never really said anything nice to me ever. Everything she does is like a favour. Like I need to be grateful that she decided to live with me. She fully depends on me financially. And behaves like it's another favour. She doesn't like to ask, Ms. Princess. So I suggested we open a joint account in the international bank down the road. But no, she wanted me to deposit money every month in hers. Why bother with all those formalities, she argued. I gave in because I wanted her to feel comfortable. But man, she spends. How or on whom? I have no clue. None of her friends or family visits us. I don't think she keeps in regular touch with them either. I asked her a few times. And she blamed that one on me. She said they can't stand me and therefore. Excuse me, how is it my fault if her parents don't respect her decision? I wonder how she spends the money, though. Don't mistake me. I am not grudging that. In fact, I believe that a man's primary responsibility towards his woman and family is that of a provider. I enjoy that role. It gives me a sense of control, a sense of power. I also am proud of the fact that I built my business from scratch. That too, gives me a sense of accomplishment. I consider myself lucky in business but what I can't figure out is why my personal life has been so unsatisfying. I do my best and yet the women in my life have no respect or value for it. One bore my children and left me and this one is the limit. She happens to be my wife but is so aloof, so distant, always talks of privacy and space. What's going on? Will somebody help me understand? Of late, my BP has been acting up. And the doctor has increased my insulin dosage too. Sometimes, when I see my sons growing up without my involvement, my ex-wife treating me like a contagious disease and the current one on her own trip, all I want to do is end this farce called life. I haven't mentioned this to anybody but I am on anti-depressants and sedatives. And of course, alcohol, my most reliable saviour...

Prabhat

I am 32, I love dogs, I love bikes, I love working out, I love my work and I love men. Yes, you heard it right. I am differently inclined. It's so normal these days, did you say? You know many such people and they're great human beings, did you say? And the best of creative geniuses are non conformists, did you say? You know what? Only the last two are true. Being different from the rest of your society is still a big deal and no, nobody considers it normal, yet. At least in India. All through my teenage, I struggled to understand my awkward urges and fought them. I even tried going against my nature to fit in. But nothing worked. Finally, I had no choice but to accept that this is who I am. And who I am, is different from who they are. I mean the 'normal' men. Why are we not allowed to be ourselves if we are different from the rest of the world, I wonder. Even though I have come to terms with myself, I haven't yet come out in the open. I don't have the guts to. Also I feel that would be really selfish because I belong to a traditional, south Indian family. My mother would die of embarrassment and grief, somehow blaming herself for how I turned out. My father would pretend I was never born. So, being open about my true self is not an option for me. But my sister knows. And yes, she has been incredibly understanding. That's the best part about her. She lives by her own rules. And doesn't wait for a helping hand to pick her up if she falls down along the way. She had married a man of her choice, much against my parents' will when she was just 22 and now she is married to another man, again of her choice.

I had never been very involved in her life, caught up that I was in my own personal drama but I truly cared for her always. I got close to her recently. I must admit, I don't like the way her current husband, Dev, treats her. I have been visiting her often, of late, out of concern for her and I must confess, I feel she will be better off without him. He is a moneyed man and I am not sure if he will let her live in peace as long as he is alive. By the way, I haven't told you something very important about myself. I don't believe killing cockroaches amounts to cruelty against animals.

Yadagiri

I am a gardener in Menaka Madam and Dev Saab's household. I am a natural when it comes to plants and gardening. And madam respects me, I know that. Along with my wife Rani and my three daughters. Look at my bad luck. All my children are daughters. Rani and I prayed at every temple to be blessed with a son each time she was pregnant but God wasn't very kind to us. Madam gets very upset when I say this to her. She says, "Yadgiri, don't ever think like that. Women are Goddesses. Nowadays we have women police officers, bureaucrats, ministers, business tycoons. Make sure your children study well. And don't worry about anything." I keep quiet. How can I argue with her? She is the one who has admitted my daughters to the English medium school even though it's costly. But I know what a curse it is to be born a girl in downtrodden communities like ours. Nothing ever changes for us. Nobody marries our girls without dowries. Later if they are lucky they get three meals a day and stay home to look after their children. Or else they work as domestic help in some rich man's home to support their husbands. Look at my wife, Rani. Her name means queen! All she has done her whole life is to work in people's homes. Sweeping, swabbing, washing vessels, clothes… When she lived with her parents she worked to help them. Now, she does to help me. I feel so guilty whenever I look at her rough palms and feet full of corns and cracks. But she never complains. She is more accepting of fate than I am. Not that we have any choice. Back home – we belong to the same village in Karimnagar – there has been a drought ever since we've opened our eyes to see the world. We're actually lucky. With the money we have earned in the city, we've been able to dig a borewell in the backyard of my parents' home. At least, they don't have to struggle for water. We also send money to my old parents so they can eat peacefully. The situation of other people in our community is worse. They have no jobs, no farm yields, no food to eat, no water to drink; two pairs of clothes have to last three months. Somehow, they get along with their daily wages from working as labourers at construction sites. Even there women are sexually exploited by the supervisors or landlords. Men are beaten up if they protest. The world may have made huge progress in science and technology but they haven't found a cure for hunger yet. Hunger is the disease that makes us put up with every other form of abuse.

We – Rani, our children and I – are lucky to have this job which gives us food, clothing and shelter. That's why Rani keeps telling me to shut up when I get into one of those moods of bemoaning our fate. Mostly, I agree with her but at times when she has to choose between my children and her job and she is forced to choose the latter, my blood boils with helplessness. Like recently, my youngest daughter had some virus attack. She couldn't open her eyes because of the high temperature and hadn't eaten for two days. The doctor had told us to make sure she gets enough fluids or she may get dehydrated. Just when Rani was somehow getting her to drink electral, Saab yelled at the top of his voice calling out for Rani. She just dumped the half conscious girl involuntarily and ran up. My little daughter collapsed on the floor. I had gone out to the pharmacy to get medicines. This was the sight that greeted me as I was stepping into the house. Rani dropping the kid with a thud and running upstairs. That's the moment I hated myself, my life, my wife's helplessness and Saab's inhumane behaviour. This one is a mild instance. At others, he has abused me with the filthiest expletives if he felt I didn't mow the lawn when I had to or didn't do something the way he expected me to or did something the way he didn't want it…The reasons were a million but his reaction was unfailingly the same. Only the degree of his rage varied. If I was lucky, I got away with verbal abuses or he would beat me up mercilessly. Madam comes and apologises every time. She gives us money, gifts, sweets for my kids, saris for my wife, slippers for me, something or the other, to make us feel better. It's not just with us; Saab is the same with every other employee. Even his accountant. Unlike us, the poor old man is educated but even then. It's only because of madam, people work in this house. God forbid, if she goes away sometime like his other wife did, then God help him…I heard that madam left her husband to marry Saab. What kind of a woman would want to marry this maniac? Unless of course, she had been married to a worse guy. God alone knows, what goes on in these big people's homes…

The other day when he started raising his voice and yelling at madam, I lost my temper. Of late, he has been screaming often at her. She walks away quietly, with just a few calm words, usually. They speak in English all the time but I can understand a few words. One day after she had left the house, Saab uttered loudly to himself, "Bitch, what does she think of herself?" That day I wanted to kill him. I just felt like picking up the axe from the back yard and chopping his head off. Even I was surprised at my rage. But that's the depth of my anger against this cruel man and respect for my kind madam.

Chapter III

Think before you make a wish; it might just come true…

She stood in front of the aquarium looking at the gold fish glide through the water; bright, orange, busy with nothing to do except swim the length and breadth of their world confined by human fancy. She looked around the house that seemed gray and dusty. The plants she had grown in the pots had withered, for want of nourishment and attention. The doors and the windows were shut tight. Not even a hint of wind flickered indoors. Except for the buzz of their old gigantic refrigerator and the drone of the aquarium, an intense stillness loomed large. As if life had come to a stand still.

The dining room was spartan; the table looked deserted. In the living room where she was standing now, the sofas mourned for the lost companionship of two people who were a couple not so long ago. Everything seemed rather forlorn. The only bright things were the cushions – bright red spots in the solemnity of a black and white décor. The old grandfather's clock had stopped ticking, the little cuckoo in it still, provoking her to contemplate on her life, on how things were and how they could have been if she had let them be.

"What are you looking at?" He managed to startle her.

"House looks so dead, don't you think?" she smiled sadly as she replied with a question.

"Well, it is. I have no doubts. There's only one thing alive here and that's me," he replied flashing a toothy grin. He had a dazzling, clean, white set. She wondered how they could remain untouched by the nicotine he inhaled like oxygen. Even now she found his smile as endearing as she had in the past. Except for a while, when she abhorred every minute aspect of him.

"And you used to say you would die without me," she said, teasing, mocking, arms around his neck, "Look at you, alive and throbbing, even after being away from me for three years."

"Shut up," he said sealing her lips with his. She could feel his eagerness for her. Nothing much had changed. In fact, nothing had changed. Except the fact that he was no longer her husband and she, was somebody else's wife. He didn't let her think any more. They kissed hungrily. He knew exactly how to navigate around her body. He knew where to touch her. He knew just what to do. He knew how to make her breathless. He just knew. He knew every single thing about her. He even knew what kind of pain gave her pleasure. He sucked on the nape of her neck and she felt she was in heaven. This was heaven. The heaven that had seemed lifeless to her a few years ago, when she had walked out on him unable to come to terms with his indifference. That's how it had seemed then. How wrong she was! How could she, how could she ever have doubted his love for her? But she had. And she was paying for it with her mind, her body, her soul, with life itself.

She looked at the man smoothening her tresses through tear-hazed eyes. "Remember, you always wished you were my lover. So there." She laughed aloud. He even knew what to say when. It was she who didn't know what she would be losing when she was throwing it all away. "God knows why I said that. We seriously need to think before we wish for something. Your mother always told me the words you utter during the twilight hour have the power of coming true. How I wish I could turn the clock back," she said looking at her wristwatch, "I better go." She sat up. "When do I see you again?" he asked, pulling her back into his arms. She left much later. Just before leaving, she looked into his eyes and said, "If given a second chance, I'll come back to you forever." Outside the apartment, over the Tank Bund, the sun was setting. The hour was twilight.

Menaka had said that to Rishi but she knew it wasn't that simple. The man she had left Rishi for, her current husband, Dev, was one hell of a complicated guy. She had discovered one such aspect of his personality soon after their marriage. On the night of their wedding day, to be precise. His son from his first marriage, Karan, had come over to attend his dad's marriage. Late in the evening, few of their friends had dropped in for a drink. Somehow, 8-year-old Karan had cut his forefinger that shed two and a half drops of blood. The maid was summoned for the wound to be cleaned and bandaged. The doting dad supervised the entire operation all the while instructing the maid what to do and how to do it. It was quite obvious from the maid's expression that such fuss over minor incidents was most common in Saab's household.

One by one all the guests made their exit. Dev and Menaka walked Karan to his room and tucked him in his bed. Just as the dad gave a good night peck and was about to leave, Karan began whining. Menaka consoled the child and he would have surely settled down, had Dev not butted in and began fussing over him. After watching the father-son enact a battle front-wounded soldier drama for a good 15 minutes, Menaka muttered good night and went into their bedroom expecting Dev to join her once the kid had gone off to sleep. Dev did join her after half an hour but with Karan in tow. That's how the three of them spent their wedding night, cramped in one bed. She couldn't sleep a wink. She hadn't tossed and turned either. She just lay there staring at the ceiling. She wouldn't probably have minded it all that much, had it not been the reason she had remarried for. For conversation. For togetherness. But what's not to be will not be. You can run away from people but there's no way out of situations. She had changed men in the hope of changing circumstances but her life had remained the same. The man who had pursued her relentlessly, who had persuaded her to stray, was fast asleep in the same bed untouched by her presence. What had she gotten into? Was it going to be the proverbial case of frying pan to fire? She didn't have to wait long to find out...

Chapter IV

Life's the only classroom in which you learn a lesson after giving the test...

Such a fine line between love and hatred, Rishi thought as he lit a cigarette, after Menaka had left. All through their married life he was subjected to her swinging moods, unfailingly. The line blurred without a warning with stunning outbursts that left him stunned. She swung from a sweet nice mood to a terrible one with amazing dexterity, like the thunder that inevitably followed the flash of a lightning. It was scary, initially, the way her behaviour would change drastically. One moment they would be sharing a joke, laughing their heads off and the very next moment she would be ready to bite his head off, accusing him of insensitivity over some inane remark he would have made. Okay, agreed, he had never tried to make her understand his point of view. But that was not because he didn't care, he just didn't know how to respond to her mercurial moods. How could you be making glorious out-of-this-world love one moment and be spitting fire, hurling abuses the next? How could anybody do that? And why? But Menaka did. And he was never able to figure out why everything he said was held against him. The intensity that scared him also had him addicted to her. To her love and to her fury. She was like the cigarette he smoked. He knew it was bad for him and yet the first thing he reached out to, as soon as he opened his eyes, was his morning fix. Of the nicotine and of her. The former damaged his lungs, the latter, his heart. Yet, the thought of giving up either had never occurred to him. But it had occurred to her. One wretched evening, as he was switching on the TV after an abandoned effort to kiss her

41

(You stink like an ashtray, she'd said pushing him away), she threatened to walk out if he didn't kick the habit. He laughed it off and lit one, just to spite her. A week later the joke was on him, when she announced, out of the blue, rather matter-of-factly that she was leaving. By the time it registered and before he could bring himself to respond, she was gone. He hadn't a clue when she had packed her things or where she was going. The first two days he thought it would pass, she would get over her anger like she always did and call. He even tried hard to quit smoking. He had reduced the number of cigarettes to half. On the fourth day, when she called, he tried telling her that but she cut him off mid sentence, "Listen Rishi, meet me at the lawyer's," and gave him the address. Once again she had stunned him with her unpredictability. The same unpredictability that had appealed to him immensely when they had met had turned out to be his nemesis that day. He knew he didn't deserve it. He promised himself that he would talk her out of it. After all, how could she throw away something they had shared for a decade? Surely, she was acting on a whim. It couldn't be his smoking that had spoilt everything they ever shared. Can't be. But then, he couldn't put it past her to behave so irrationally. She was by all means highly impulsive. That's how they had married. On an impulse. She was 22 and he was 28 when she had walked out of her father's house only because the old man had said that she deserved better and landed up at his bachelor dump one stormy night. They had been inseparable since then. She had converted his dingy one bedroom apartment into a cosy, lovers' den. That's when he had realized that money had nothing to do with tasteful living. He was a struggling artist and she was his inspiration. On the first evening after they had gotten married, he wanted to sketch her. She was game. Those days she was game for anything. He sketched her with a back brush. Right arm in the air. Elbow against the window. Hair on the left shoulder outlined by rays of light. Head tilted to the side. Line of the cheek against her hair. Bee stung lips. Eyes wide open. Come hither expression. Luscious breasts. She drove him mad. Born man eater. He didn't know whether he should devour her first or finish the sketch. He did both eventually. She was the only girl for him in the world. And she was equal to a harem. Insatiable and he never knew which one he had to deal with at any given point.

They'd had their spats even then but she had somehow understood at the end of them all. She was a handful, his wife. God, she was something else. Luckily for them, their raging hormones and their undersized single bed only added up. When their bodies spoke to each other, their minds surrendered. They were inseparable like Siamese twins or so he thought. She had not shown the slightest inclination to spend time away from him even for a night. There was never a question of 'space' and 'me time' as far as the two of them were concerned. Every available free moment, they had been together. At least, that's how he had seen it.

Only a few months ago, she had begun showing signs of being seriously rattled with him. She seemed to be having a whole lot of nightmares these days. She had narrated one such to him once when he had returned home in the wee hours of the morning about some scary person warning her that if she didn't leave him, she would have to face death. He had put it down to her anxiety about his late return. But whatever he said or did, she found fault with. He would flare up whenever she criticized him or his actions. Which was most of the time they were together. The rest, she sulked. The reasons for which ranged from the wet bathroom floor, disgusting cigarette stink to his working late. He was dismissive. Honestly speaking, he was inure to her erratic behaviour. That's where he had misjudged her. It had nothing to do with something as trivial as his smoking. It was much more serious like her having found a lover. Like it always happens, he was the last to know. That too, only after he had signed the divorce papers. And that too, when she had told him. When he had tried his best to make her understand, begged, pleaded, cried, and she remained unfazed, he realized that there was no point in it any more. He had agreed for a mutual consent divorce. Since there were no children involved and no maintenance issues, it had taken less than a month for the court to grant Menaka what she wanted. Even before they entered the court on the day of the hearing, Rishi kept telling her, "What the hell are we doing here? Let's just turn back and forget that we'd ever been here." But she stuck fast. He kept asking her where she was staying; she ignored his question completely as if she hadn't heard him. Only after the deed was done with, when they were walking towards their respective cars, he repeated the question and she asked him back bitterly, "Are you concerned or curious?" God, why did she always get him wrong? Why did she always miss the point? He had presumed she was staying at one of her friends' or her mother's, and since he'd thought she needed time away from him to cool off, he hadn't bothered her with incessant calls and texts, and here she was giving it the colour of indifference.

Once again she had cut him off when he tried explaining, "I thought..." "Never mind. Who cares what you think any way? I'm living in with Dev. And yes, we're lovers. It might not make any difference to you but I'm telling you." That day he experienced the true meaning of words like 'shattered', 'heartbroken' and other such words associated being dumped and left in the lurch. From living life as a married man to existing with painful solitude, the transition was sudden. He would bawl initially, whenever he was home. He missed her like crazy. Gradually, he had hardened. He had made truce with life but his sex life had grounded to a halt. Something had snapped in his system. Though he did wake up with a painful hard on at times, he just couldn't bring himself to have sex with another woman. Life had taught him another lesson – making love and having sex were two different things. Life's perhaps the only classroom where you learn a lesson after giving the test. And he'd learnt that he was incapable of the latter after a disastrous attempt at a dalliance with a colleague. Priyamvada had always given him 'the look' even when he was married but he'd had no inclination whatsoever to be with another woman. In fact, his male friends poked fun at him many times over such incidents. Now, after she had come to know that he had been divorced, she had most eagerly invited him to her house ostensibly for a meal. As things normally turn out the way they do when a single man visits an interested woman, they had landed on the sofa in a horizontal position while watching TV. That's when disaster struck. His body refused to cooperate. Despite more than a hint of cleavage on show and tantalising perfume, the works. Poor Priyamvada was most understanding and moved him and herself to the sprawling bed in the hope that space would bring out the better side of him. But nothing helped. In fact, he didn't even feel the slightest inkling to kiss her, even though his ego hurt that he couldn't rise to the occasion.

Strangely, whenever he thought of HER, that wretched infidel, his body responded – WHAM! His sex life had been fucked up by his ex wife. He was beyond repair now. To hell with her! This is what happens when you marry the one you ever loved. Oh God! Why couldn't he have made her stay? Why couldn't it have lasted like countless other marriages? He'd resigned himself to his reality, until recently. And then, something dramatic happened! Amazingly, his sex life began to roar once again. After he met a very special person who took over the reins of his life. He was filled with gratitude when he should have been full of despise for letting her do as she pleased with him. For, the special person was his ex-wife. She had walked back into his life as stunningly as she had walked out. And there he was – ready and waiting. He owed it to her for restoring normalcy to his dysfunctional life. He hated her for dumping and picking him up at her convenience. She had walked into his office shamelessly one afternoon, coolly like nothing had happened. As if they were college buddies who had lost touch. From then on, she had taken over his life again.

The first time – the second time around – had left him both exhilarated and exasperated. There was an instant chemical reaction when they had touched. It was a familiar but powerful erotic sensation – hot and blinding. He wanted to say, stop, you've no right to my body. Instead, he loved what the woman he detested was doing to him. Almost objectifying him. But he needed her. Like a claustrophobic man needs space. I am in trouble, he said to himself. He was falling into her. All over again. And he was wallowing in it. Shamelessly. Despite himself. He almost died of gratitude when she rode him bringing him to a mind-numbing climax, finishing him off. Make it last forever, he pleaded and immediately wished he had bitten his tongue off. Or better still killed himself. God, how he hated her for the ease with which she ruled over him. He realized with a pang that he had just been had. What a cold-blooded bitch. But man, was she hot!

Body is a good adviser but a bad ruler. In her presence, like in the past, his body had no use for good counsel. The pleasure did not last forever. It seemed like an eternity, though.

Chapter V

Life's lived forwards but understood backwards...

When they'd met, Menaka hadn't considered Rishi her type. He was of medium height, thin and wheatish. She liked tall, well-built, fair guys. But once he began speaking, everything came undone. She noticed from closer quarters that he had a fine, lithe physique and animal-like vigour. There was something about him that drew her overwhelmingly. Inexplicably. Just to see him move about was a pleasure. His eyebrows were light, his forehead way too broad for his face. But when he smiled, his eyes lit up. His personality overshadowed his looks. His easy charm and frankness more than made up for his lack of conventional good looks.

They'd met while hosting a program for a radio station. He had a sexy voice; the kind that made her dreamy. His was one of the most heard music countdown programs on the radio. It was mesmeric. Girls loved him. They hovered around him all the time. She didn't like the idea of being one of them. But she was smitten by him, his repertoire of words, his knowledge of music, of books, of everything that appealed to her. She liked to believe he was a passing fancy, though.

That night while having dinner, she wondered what kind of food he liked.

Who?

Rishi.

Rishi who?

That's right. She wasn't thinking about him.

Was she?

Who cared what he liked? At least she didn't. Right. Nevertheless, she phoned him when she returned to her room. And she remembered his number without checking the piece of paper on which he had jotted it down for her. There was no reply. No one home? Did he live alone? Damn. She couldn't resist the urge to keep trying his phone. Just before she drifted off, she thought, tomorrow, I'll call him first thing in the morning. Tomorrow…Give him a ring… May be…

Menaka was reliving the stirrings of their initial days as she drove back from Rishi's apartment to her house. So typical of her to resist her own feelings. Almost rejecting them in the process. Always living in a state of self-denial. Suddenly, she realized she hadn't touched up her lipstick in the hurry to leave. She pulled up the car to a side and halted. Quickly, she removed her compact from her handbag and took a thorough look at herself in the mirror. All the signs of having made passionate love were undoubtedly there. With trembling fingers she managed to fix the kohl and applied a fresh coat of lipstick. It was more or less okay now. Even if it wasn't, there was not much she could do about it. She felt like crying at the irony of her situation. Nobody, no other woman would or could be in a situation like hers. Sick, that she had to feel guilty about something that was her reality not too long ago. What great knack she had to create situations that were stupidly one-of-their-kind. She tried focusing on the traffic. Just the thought of getting back home was putting her off. Fuck, what have I gone and done, she said to herself. If only she could just turn back and get to where she had come from. At some point, this had to stop. Either she had to put her past behind her and accept her present or make her past her present and erase the present like it had never been present. Too complicated and confusing!

Were there some elements in her that were in opposition, tearing her apart? If she could find a balancing point, or a hinge between the two polarized elements, there may still be hope of mending the conflict but right now, she carried a certain tragedy on her, something like immense pain. Was she consciously bringing in restlessness and turmoil into her life? Or was this simply a non-workable situation? It was time for her to separate exaggeration and even rationalization from the truth.

Chapter VI

When you're not in alignment with your true self, you disintegrate...

When she reached home, she was greeted by a frowning Dev at the entrance. His brows were perpetually knotted like the world strove to displease him all the time. He looked at her seriously, with angry eyes. He was always serious and stiff and somehow reduced her to the same condition when she was with him. God knows what she had seen in him! She just put one step outside the car and he asked in his trademark stern tone, "Where were you? How many times do I have to tell you not to switch off your mobile phone when you're out of the house?" She got out of the car and when she was locking the door, he repeated his questions, adding another one. "Can't you keep me informed about your whereabouts?"

"Do you tell me about yours?"

"Well, you never ask."

"So why don't you stop asking too?"

"Just because you don't care doesn't mean I should stop too?"

"Neither your tone nor the look on your face seem very caring."

"What do you think it is, then?'

"Could be authority, could be suspicion, could be anything but concern."

"Ok fine. If that's what you feel, I'm never ever going to ask you again. This is the last time."

"Thanks. I do hope you stick to your word, though."

She walked past him into the house and he was left staring at her butt that jutted provocatively from her tight jeans. How he hated her style of dressing! His attempts at getting her to dress the way he liked had met with utter disregard from her.

It worried him – her behaviour. Of late, she was getting increasingly distant. He was beginning to get scared of her moods. He wondered if she was planning to leave him and get back with that loser ex-husband of hers. What had that man given her? She had had to work hard all through her first marriage to live the way she wished to. She had never said it in so many words but he had gathered it during their conversations before their marriage. His heart would go out to her when he had seen her working so hard. For Dev, everything translated into money. As far as he was concerned, if a woman worked, it had to be for the money. Not that it was a conscious thought. Neither was it his fault. He just didn't know any different. He belonged to an extremely wealthy family. Well educated but feudal. No woman in his family had ever worked. Or considered a career. All of them studied at premier institutions, acquired the best degrees money could buy. MAs, M.BAs and what have you. In economics, literature, finance, name it. But career for the women in the family was never a consideration. The only women who worked in his extended family were the ones who 'assisted' their husbands. Not that they were condescending in any manner towards a woman. It was just the way things had always been in their families. In cases where the girls didn't find suitable grooms till their late 20s, they would enroll for an additional catering or interior designing course to enhance their house keeping skills which would come in handy eventually when they did get married.

Dev had been the most liberal in his entire family. When he had 'let' his first wife work, his cousins were of the opinion, "Dev is very broad-minded. He is 'allowing' his wife to work." Dev's chest expanded with pride when he heard such remarks. He would often tell Vaidehi, "You've no idea how lucky you're. Men in our families are not as open minded as I am." Shocked beyond words that such mind sets prevailed in this day and age, Vaidehi would be speechless and Dev would ignorantly mistake it for silent agreement. For most part, Vaidehi preferred silence to words because her sensibilities told her that this one man was beyond reasoning. That continued to be her stance during their fifteen years of marriage. Which is why Dev was completely baffled when they split. "We'd never had any problems. I can't understand what went wrong." He would tell his friends.

By nature, Vaidehi was a non-confrontational person. Even the manner in which they split was most peaceful. As it happened, they had been living in a rented bungalow since their marriage. When they had decided to build their own house on Dev's ancestral land, Vaidehi had no role to play. Like always, he planned every detail. Yes, he did keep her informed about it. It took him a good one-year to build the house. When he saw the final outcome, Dev was ecstatic. He said to Vaidehi, "Finally, my sons will live in their own house. It's turned out exactly the way I had imagined. My dream house." Vaidehi smiled like she always did but not without observing how he said 'my sons', 'my dream house.' That's how it had always been in their relationship. Every single decision, whether it concerned him, their children or even her, was his. She never had a say. Sometimes, when she did try to say something he just trashed her opinion. Initially, she would cry every time he vetoed whatever she suggested. But now, it didn't matter. She neither expressed her viewpoint nor was concerned about his.

Vaidehi was an army officer's daughter. Colonel Murthy was a democrat. He always involved his wife and daughters in every decision that concerned him or their house. There had never been a question of 'it's my life' or 'none of your business' kind of attitude. Everything concerning everybody was everybody's concern. Coming from where she did, confrontation was alien to her. She knew how to negotiate a disagreement, she did, but with Dev, there was no such need. He never gave any credence to her beliefs or opinions.

A similarity with her father had sparked initial interest in Dev. He'd come across as pretty responsible, attentive even. At 28, he was every bit his own man. It had impressed her greatly. When he had popped the question on his birthday, she had asked him for time to think it over. Definitely, she was not head over heels in love with him. She wasn't greatly attracted to him physically, either. She confided in her mother who said, "I think, he's a decent enough guy. Obviously he's in love with you. He's also independent and seems to have a great future ahead. Talk to him clearly about what you're looking for in a marriage and if he's open to it, I see no reason why you should say no." Vaidehi thought in any case she had to marry some day. Instead of getting into a marriage that would be arranged by her parents, this was probably a better choice. They had a chat and she told him that work was an important aspect of her life. There was no question of quitting and staying home. He'd agreed readily. So it was settled, then. That's how their relationship had been. Well thought out and meticulously executed.

Dev was a very 'proper' guy. Everything in his life had to be carefully considered and planned perfectly. Her bridal sari was chosen by him, even the make-up artist, like every other detail of their wedding. She had been amused but felt pampered at the same time.

After they got married and started living together, she realized there was one major difference between her father and him. Dev's decision was his, nobody had a say in it. It didn't even occur to him to consult others. That one difference had nullified every other similarity in their personalities.

Her married life had been a confusing affair from pretty early on. She had certain expectations from their relationship and they were never met. He bought her the most expensive clothes and jewellery, took her out to classy dinners and luxury holidays. But there was something jarringly amiss and she was too stunned by his dominating ways. She consoled herself saying that these were initial adjustment problems. There were times though when she would seethe for days. Anger is the first alerting signal that your personal space is being invaded. And if you don't express it, chances are you're closing the doors to self-discovery. Failing to recognize the source of an emotion, flares it up in another part of the psyche. But Vaidehi neither expressed her anger nor did she recognize the cause. She only suppressed it. Also, since she wasn't equipped with the will to assert herself or voice her dissent, she learnt to go along with his plans. Sometimes, she even psyched herself into thinking that he knew better. But it still hurt her when issues that meant a world to her were not even acknowledged by him. Like the time when he had decided the names of their two sons, the school they would go to, the kind of clothes they wore, the kind of food they should eat and stuff like that. He even decided what clothes she should wear when she went out with him or to work. In any case, he chose almost all her outfits except the ones that were gifted by her friends or family. He would land at her workplace ostensibly to fetch her and announce enroute, "We're going shopping for your clothes. Or I feel like buying jewellery for you today." And wait for her response. She had even trained herself to appear pleased to please him as best as she could. But he would often flare up at her 'nearly damp reaction.' "Why do you always look so disinterested in everything?" Bull's eye. The truth was exactly that – she had never been the kind to go orgasmic over clothes or jewellery. She did like ethnic stuff – handlooms and silver jewellery - but he thought nothing of them. She had learnt to appreciate chiffons, silks and diamonds over the years.

There are those who know how to stand their ground and voice their opinions. And then there are those who never voice their opinions therefore the need to stand their ground doesn't arise. Vaidehi had moulded herself to fit into the latter though in her parents' home, she belonged to the former category. And when you are not in alignment with your true self, you're bound to disintegrate at some point.

Her parents had taught her to have a mind of her own but completely ignored the need to tell her how vital it was to get your point across. Sometimes there are arguments, at times there are disagreements but these are little hitches in your way if you have to assert yourself. But since she had always had her way when she was growing up without having to fight for it, Vaidehi had never felt the need to assert herself. For her, an argument meant fight and disagreement was a conflict. She hated fights and conflicts.

As far as Dev was concerned, he was an ideal husband and father. Vaidehi was his idea of a perfect wife. Always content. And why wouldn't she be? He was a good provider by any standard. He got her the best and gave her money even when she didn't ask. He never objected to her spending but she had to tell him how she spent it. He reveled being in the position of a giver. It never occurred to him how she must be taking it. Because for him, no complaints meant no problems. If only he knew how to read the signs of dissent, his marriage wouldn't have left him a devastated man.

Chapter VII

When you pretend to be what you're not; your true self revolts...

Prabhat had never been into girls. He loved their company. He had several female friends. As a matter of fact, he was always surrounded by them. Even as a kid, he hung out with girls because he felt like one of them. One day, when he tried on his sister's lacy frock and pirouetted in front of his mother, she had laughed her guts off. The second time around, when he came out with his eyes clumsily done up in her kajal, she was a li'l less amused. The third time, he added lipstick in addition to the kajal and she warned him, "Don't do that!" The fourth time when he tried on beady chains, with the kajal and lipstick, bangles and flowers in his hair that was held in place with a hair pin, she gave him one tight stinging slap across his face. Prabhat touched his cheek at the memory.

Now, he was 30, and when his mother asked him if he was dating somebody seriously, he didn't know what to tell her. "If you're not, then I'll ask Shashi Aunty to look for a nice girl for you," Rukmini said to her son, "She found this really good looking girl from a very nice family for Chintu." Chintu was his first cousin and Shashi Aunty was the neighborhood matchmaker. "No ma, not yet," he said evasively. But his mother was not the kind to give up that easily, "What do you mean, not yet? You're already 30! Tomorrow I am going to meet her," she announced gathering her knitting paraphernalia. He knew

54

what a determined little thing his old lady was. But let me cross the bridge when I come to it, he comforted himself.

Last night when his hands had brushed against his General Manager's (GM), he had felt currents running through his veins. His body heat had soared. He worked in a five star hotel as the executive assistant to the GM. Vithal, the GM was a handsome man in his forties with the body of a thirty year old. He was well built and whenever Prabhat looked at his musculature, he was mesmerized. He had heard that Vithal was a bi-sexual but he didn't know how to offer himself. Maybe, he should try meeting him alone for a drink. His last affair, which was his first one, had happened with his gym coach when he was 25. He remembered everything vividly. He had reached the gym late that day, around 11.30 in the morning. It was some holiday, yeah yeah it was the day of holi, and there was nobody in the gym. Obviously, the regulars were either busy playing with the colors or were avoiding them. The coach, Harry, was standing right behind him, helping him with the weights. Once he was done, he put the bar down and stretched himself. When he leaned backward he brushed against Harry who was still standing behind him. He looked up. That's when Harry sat next to him on the bench and kissed him on his lips. The pleasurable sensation had blown Prabhat's mind. In no time, they were at it the second time switching positions. That's when Prabhat had realized he enjoyed being at the receiving end. He was the passive one. For the next two years, they had conducted their affair clandestinely. It had reached a point when both of them were wondering if they were falling in love. That's when Harry had got this offer to be the personal trainer of some biggish film actor in Mumbai and he had left Secunderabad. For a week after Harry left, Prabhat moped. Gradually, he had come to grips with himself and life was at last back to normal. How he envied those heterosexual men! It took them such little time to find another girl if one left. He would never be that lucky. He didn't even know if he would ever be able to find a man to love and be loved. Luckily, he had met Vithal. Ever since, he was pining for him. But the whole situation was so tricky. As if being homosexual was not tough enough, he had to also deal with the fact that he had fallen for his boss. Now, when you're a man, how do you tell another man that you desire him? Had he been a woman, he could have dropped enough hints. These straight men and women had everything so easy and took it all for granted.

Now, adding to his agony was his mother's talk about marriage. He had been dreading it every time he attended a friend or cousin's wedding. But she had brought it up regularly as expected. He was hoping she would give in when he said NO. Looked like that wasn't about to happen. He contemplated if he should simply get married and try to lead a `normal' life. His mind raced back to the time when he was 20 and how revolted he had felt when a girl had kissed him. He had tried several times with other girls but nothing would happen to him. The whole campus was agog with rumors that he was impotent. When you try to pretend what you're not just to belong where you don't, your true self revolts. At the same time, he was deeply attracted to his classmate, Roshan. Every time there was physical contact with Roshan, he would want more. He felt the need to touch him, hold him, kiss him... During the nights he would have erotic dreams about Roshan. He fantasized constantly about various men, especially those Hollywood, Bollywood hunks. That's when he began reading up on the net to find an answer to his unusual feelings. When he read first person accounts of men who were different, he had no doubts left in his mind that he was one of them. For days after the self-realization, he had stifled his sobs into a pillow during the nights. With a vengeance he made out with a girl on the farewell party night. She had tried real hard to please him. Somehow he managed to get into the act and get it over with. Forget about pleasure, he didn't even feel good about the whole thing. He felt lousy. It left a bad after taste. That's when he decided that he would be celibate. He couldn't be a disgrace to his family. He couldn't be a misfit in the society. He had to camouflage his real self somehow and leave the rest to time. Maybe, in a few years everything would fall in place. Maybe, he would just wake up one fine morning and find himself attracted to girls. But nothing of the sort had happened. With each passing day, his sexuality strengthened and began waking him up to it. He just couldn't be blind to his reality any more. There was no way out but to come to terms with the fact that he was homosexual. He had agonized endlessly, though. Why the hell was he made this way? Somehow he had to get through life now. There were no hopes of 'normalcy' now. He did more research and registered himself into a support group online. Gradually, he realized that just because he didn't belong to the majority, he didn't have to be ashamed of himself. He was not abnormal. He was just different. His morale began looking up after he chatted with a few like him online. He realized he was not the only one who was going through these emotions. There were several others. That knowledge comforted him a great deal. But who was to tell the people in his world? He belonged to a regular upper middle class Telugu family. His mother had rejoiced at the birth of a boy. His grand parents were thrilled at the birth of a vamshoddharaka (the upholder/perpetuator of the family tree). Who was to tell them now, in their old age, that their vamshoddharaka was not even interested in raising a family leave alone upholding it? Would he have to live in a state of denial and obscurity for the rest of his life? Nothing can prepare a man for the realization that he can never be like other men. That he cannot do what others expect him to.

Now, if he did get married to please his parents, he would be ruining not only his but also an innocent girl's life. He had to come up with some strategy soon.

Sometimes, he toyed with the idea of letting his parents into his secret. But he knew his conventional parents would never able to handle the shock. It wasn't fair to subject them to such anguish. May be he should confide in his sister who was the more liberal kind. She had left home years ago to marry the man she loved. And then she had divorced him after a solid 10 years to marry another man. Some guts she had! He totally admired the way she led her life by her rules. She cared two hoots for people's opinions or judgments. But he was slightly wary of her moods. He could never tell how she would react. There were times when he would say something expecting her to flare up and she would laugh it off. And then there were other times when he would share something silly and she would lose her cool and give him a piece of her mind. He should visit her one of these days and check out her state of mind. That's the only way out. He was present at her second marriage as a witness from her side. Then she had invited him for lunch, which they'd had in her new fancy home with a swimming pool, gym, and the works. Her ex-husband was a regular working guy but her new one was loaded, obviously. But he knew his sister and she couldn't have fallen for money alone; there must be something about his new brother-in-law.

When he had come home and shared the idea of visiting his sister with his mother, she was pretty pissed off. Amma was definitely partial to him; she made no bones about it. "Your father had given her so much freedom right from the beginning. Look where it has got her. After ten years of marriage, that too to a man she defied us for, how can a decent woman do this? God! Can't believe she is my daughter." His mother and sister had never gotten along right from the time he could remember. But their father doted on her. Nobody could say a word against her. Whenever he traveled, Prabhat was the bridge between his mother and sister.

Nanna (Telugu word for father) was really disheartened when she had walked out of the house to marry Rishi but came to terms with it soon. Over a period of time, he had developed a strong bond with his son-in-law. Even now, when Menaka and Rishi were no longer married to each other, he still kept in touch with Rishi. As far as he was concerned, once he accepted a person, the relationship was for keeps. Unless the other person decided to snap it. Prabhat had inherited the trait from his father. In every other area, he was like Amma.

When he heard the tinkering of pots and pans in the kitchen, he walked in to help his mother. It was teatime. She made these delicious savory stuff to snack with tea. He saw her mixing the besan batter for some aloo bajjis and said, "Ma, let me do it." He loved cooking. He actually wanted to do a course in hotel management to be a chef but due to sheer peer pressure had studied B.Com and followed it up with an M.BA. Luckily, he had secured his first job in a five star hotel. He wasn't any where near the kitchen but he was happy to be part of the hospitality industry. Amma replied, "Na I'll do it. You sit and chat with me. Whoever marries you will be one lucky girl ra kanna." She referred to his interest in cooking. There she goes again! "Ma, why should I get married at all? Can't I stay a bachelor forever? Consider this, you don't have to put up with another woman in this house, there won't be any daily khit-pit. You've no idea how these modern girls are. They are very independent and don't appreciate any interference in their affairs."

"All that is fine. But I've to do my duty as a mother, na kanna. How long will you stay alone?"

"Where am I alone? You and nanna are with me."

"I meant without a partner. Things should happen at the right age. If you don't marry soon, people will start thinking there is something wrong with you. Moreover, you'll also start feeling lonely. Your nanna and I are your parents. You'll feel the need for a wife. Why, what is your problem in getting married? Tell me."

"Nothing in particular. Just that I feel happier this way."

"Yeah, yeah. You'll say this now. Once your wife comes, you will forget me too.'

"Never, ma. You're my true love." He placed his hands on her shoulders and stood behind her watching the golden brown bajjis float on the oil. For Prabhat, his mother was the world. Everybody and every thing else came secondary. He would come running into the house from school looking for her if she wasn't waiting for him outside the gate. He would clutch her hand and go rat-a-tat about every single thing that transpired at school. A habit that seemed to be disappearing of late.

"Acha, tell me about your office," she asked out of the blue, "These days you don't tell me anything."

Suddenly, Prabhat felt very self-conscious. How on earth could he tell her that he had a crush on his boss?

"Why are you so quiet? Are you having problems?"

"Oh no, ma. Everything is perfect. It's the same routine everyday. Nothing special."

And then his father got back home. The three of them got busy discussing which they preferred more – aloo bajjis or onion pakodas. They couldn't come to a consensus but Prabhat was relieved that the subject of his marriage was dropped in the process. He had no clue that his relief was short lived, that his mother had already made concrete plans for him and that his life would soon be out of his control…

Chapter VIII

Nothing or nobody needs to be fixed. Everything is the way it ought to be...

In her early childhood, Menaka had found her mother either too indulgent or too strict depending on her mood and what she was doing at a given moment. This unreliability and unpredictability translated to a sense of distrust in Menaka that deepened, as she grew older. The antipathy they shared would fade out when her father was around. She confided in him that she just wasn't comfortable with Amma. He contemplated for a while and said, "Listen baby, the best gift we can give ourselves is to accept people for what they are. Especially in close relationships. Try to look at it from her point of view. Parents tend to go overboard only because they care. You mother means well, she might appear to you like she doesn't understand but believe me, she does. How can she not? You're her daughter, her first born. Agreed, she gets carried away, but that's only because she loves you. Yes, there are times when she's pretty irrational and unreasonable but what to do?"

It hadn't comforted her all that much.

"But nanna, most of the times she is totally wrong, I'm sure you know it. Why don't you try to change her?"

"There is nothing like right or wrong in human beings, okay? Never judge people by your definitions. Now, how do you know that you're right and she's

60

wrong? If you ask her, she will say just the opposite. The worst crime we can ever commit is to try to change someone to suit your needs."

She wasn't the one to give up that easily. "But if it's for somebody's good, then?"

"Let me repeat. There is nothing right or wrong. Everything is in your perception... have you heard that before? Get over your need to change people. Nothing or nobody needs to be fixed. Everything is the way it should be. Get this into your little head and keep it there. It'll do you a lot of good."

"So, now what are you trying to do? Aren't you advising me what's good for me?"

"I plead guilty your honour. By the way, you'll make an excellent lawyer."

They'd both laughed.

"Having said that, let me tell you what makes us most unhappy is our need to change the world around us. We are constantly driven by the need to correct others or advise them on what's right or what's wrong. And when our advice goes unheeded, we become miserable. Now, would you change yourself if your mother asked you to? Obviously not. Because, according to you, you're right. Now, who gives us the right to change others? I don't know if I am making any sense to you right now. But some day you'll understand what I'm saying."

But like she had read somewhere 'Life is lived forwards but understood backwards.' She understood now as she remembered the conversation she had had with her father when she was 17 or 18. Such wisdom obviously hadn't made sense to her then. Now, she could put a finger on what had ruined her relationship with Rishi. The breaking point came when she began feeling the need to change him. Her instant flaring up every time she felt he behaved like an average person, her outbursts at his lack of ambition, her constant need to push him...that what was her undoing. What was the point thinking about it now? She had already committed the crime. She had already caused a great deal of unhappiness. Now what?

Sometimes, she thought Rishi had come into her life to attune her to her own needs and longings. Sometimes a person comes into your life not so that you can possess them but to stimulate exquisite feelings that better acquaint you with your heart's desires. An unfulfilled relationship is not a terrible thing. In fact, its effect can enrich your other relationships. She should try not to cheapen such feelings by trying to possess him. Even when she was with him, he had never made her feel like he belonged to her. Though she had believed that she belonged to him. Ideally, she should let go of him – he was just a symbol. Ideally, she should let go of the symbol for the sake of the essence. Ideally, she should move on. In any case, it was she who had opted out. Why then was she unable to leave him in the true sense? She could rationalize everything, she had always been able to, but to give up on him totally wasn't something she was even willing to consider.

When she had left him, she hadn't understood how deeply bound she was to him. She had believed that she could replace him with another man who seemed better and she would never ever feel the need for him. It sounded like the best way out of a relationship that was going nowhere. But ironically, Dev had made her realize what Rishi meant to her. Instead of forgetting him in Dev's presence, she thought of him all the more.

Every time Dev said or did something, she compared it to how Rishi would say or do the same thing. And each time Rishi emerged the winner. She knew it wasn't fair to compare the two. It was like comparing a strawberry to a banana. Dev was like the exotic strawberry. Strawberry was good as a topping but banana was a whole meal in itself. And she had tossed it in the garbage can thinking she would never need it again. Once the novelty of being with Dev had worn off, she was craving Rishi again. How could she have underestimated her attachment of a decade? He had become a part of her system. Every morning she woke up expecting to see Rishi next to her and when she saw Dev, her heart sank. The impact of her drastic action sunk in. And she felt bogged down with the realisation. She couldn't understand herself at all. She blamed Rishi for being a loser. Why couldn't he have put his foot down firmly and stopped her from leaving? She would die to speak to him.

In saner moments, when she relived her relationship with Rishi, she realized that she hadn't ever felt a deep sense of satisfaction ever. He always left her longing and feeling unfulfilled. They always had glorious love making sessions but she wanted to be held and soothed later. Instead, he would light up, take a deep drag and say, "The most satisfying smoke is after great sex." He never noticed her expression of disappointment. Though physically she was satiated, emotionally she was left untouched.

There were other times when she would rush home to share something important or exciting with him. "Guess what happened today," she would say and he would be like, "Just wait. Let me finish this first." The tasks he had on hand were always most mundane. By the time he was done with his preoccupation, she would have lost interest. Not that he asked her ever what was it that she wanted to share with him. On stray occasions when he remembered to, after several hours had passed, she would say, "Forget it!" in anger and he promptly would. She couldn't blame him, could she? After all, he was only following her instructions. Yet, she repeated it day after day. Every day she felt rejected, her feelings disregarded. What kind of a masochistic woman was she? Or was she optimistic? Did she love the pain she caused herself or was she being hopeful that he would respond to her the way she wanted him to? Whatever it was, she felt so out of sync with him. And she didn't like the feeling. She wanted to be one with him. She wanted him to feel for her the way she felt for him. At the same time, she knew how capable he was of making her feel worthless and yet deep inside she felt things would change one of these days. But the day never came. It was always the same.

Of course, they had great times together. They could speak for hours about films, music, books, people. Intellectually, he stimulated her. Physically, he was a robust lover but her soul felt incomplete. A strange sense of emotional dissatisfaction pervaded her entire being. As though it was deprived of some vital nourishment. Like it was crying for attention.

Between the emotional connection we call love and its physical counterpart called sex, is a large gray area. Subconsciously, she had ventured into that chasm and felt lost in it. Now, whichever way she turned, she felt directionless. She had no clue if it was because he was disinterested in her. That wasn't entirely true. They wouldn't have come this far otherwise. But she wanted more. She wanted him to hug her, cuddle up in bed non-sexually, give her a kiss, hold her against his chest when she was worried; she wanted him to understand her instinctively. Without a need to exchange words. The only thing that was still in tact was his humour. He had an amazing knack for making people roll with laughter. Not just her. His spontaneous wise cracks and repartees had people flocking to him at gatherings. He punned almost compulsively. But even that he stretched a bit too far. He cracked his one- liners even when she was hurting or expressing some deep emotion. Like the time she had confided in him about her strained relationship with her mother and he'd quipped, "Mother of all problems." She wanted him to comfort her not come up with some smart alecky comment. The last straw was when she had noticed bleeding from her rectum and it was intensely painful. When she told him about it, groaning, he said, "And I thought I was the only painful asshole in your life." That was it. She lost it completely. She let him have it with abuses galore. "Not only are you a painful asshole, you're a complete bastard and an insensitive jerk. Now just get lost and leave me alone." How could anybody joke when some one was in pain? She sobbed uncontrollably. She could no longer tell what hurt her more – his attitude or her ailment. Even then he could have held her, apologized for being insensitive, said something to make her feel better, she would have been fine. Instead, when she stopped crying and looked up, he wasn't even there. She had somehow managed to get up and visit the doctor all by herself.

When they met in the evening, he didn't even bother to enquire how she was. She couldn't for the life of her figure out how anybody, leave alone somebody who shared your life, be so uncaring? Don't we all ask after each other's health even when we happen to be mere acquaintances? When she couldn't deal with it any more she walked into the study where he was sitting with his colleague, discussing some official matter and gave it to him like never before. She was so furious she cursed his parents, abused his upbringing, with a generous sprinkling of expletives. His colleague had bolted from the scene. Even then all he said was, "Relax, why are you getting so hyper? You scared that poor chap away." That set her off even more, "Bastard, you care more about that frigging colleague of yours than me. Are you a human being or a beast?" Even then, he didn't say what she wanted to hear. She wanted to hear him say, "I'm sorry. How are you? I have been meaning to ask you if your pain has subsided. Should we see a doctor?" If not all, at least one such thing would have made her feel instantly calmer. But no, he wouldn't say a word. He just sat there quietly, with an idiotic schoolboy look. God! He was the limit!

One night when she returned home from work, he wasn't there. She was lying down on the sofa watching TV but could barely keep her eyes open. She pressed the off button on the remote and surrendered to sleep. She forced her eyes open when she heard the bell ring. Somehow she dragged her feet groggily and opened the door expecting to see Rishi's apologetic face. Instead, she saw a hazy cloaked form who brushed her aside and walked in. In her sleepy state, by the time her mind registered what was going on, it had already settled on her sofa. She took a timid step forward but couldn't figure what this thing was. With the hollow of her stomach filling with fear, she managed, "Who are you? What do you want?" It laughed, a soft muffled mocking laughter, and replied,

"You have forgotten me? Strange! I have come here to tell you something about Rishi. No, he's not dead but he's as good as dead as far as you're concerned. He can't hear you, see you or feel you. Don't bother wasting your time trying to understand why, when and how. Just go!" She moved another step closer for a better look, despite the fear. But the form just held her by the neck and kept saying, "Go away, or I will kill you," and the grip tightened till she thought she would choke. She sat up gasping and realised she was lying down on the sofa. She had slept off without changing with her watch that showed 5 AM. Rishi wasn't back yet. As she recalled the nightmare, the bell rang and this time it WAS Rishi, thankfully. She looked at him wide eyed and he said, "Why are you looking at me as if you were not expecting to see me? Just got stuck in the editing studio," he walked in explaining. She walked behind him narrating her dream. He guffawed and shrugged it off. "You must have drifted off to sleep worrying about me. You can't get rid of me so easily babe. Look here, I am in one piece." Yeah, that must be it, she thought to herself as she headed to the kitchen to make some coffee.

Chapter IX

It doesn't matter where you are, what matters is where you wish to reach…

"People are always blaming their circumstances for what they are. I don't believe in circumstances. The people who get on in this world are the people who get up and look for the circumstances they want, and, if they can't find them, make them." Vaidehi was reading George Bernard Shaw's words and she felt he was talking to her. It had happened to her in the past too. Whenever she was looking for an answer to an issue or seeking something, she would invariably come across some passage in some book that was relevant to her situation. She felt it was a message from the universe. She was a voracious reader and books were her constant companions, right through her childhood and teens. How else could she explain this? She had read this book of famous quotes many times before but today, when she picked it up, the book opened to a page with these words. It seemed like a message. Just a while ago, she had actually begun to find fault with her circumstances -- her lack of identity in the marriage, lack of visibility in the relationship, this lack of respect… Now, she firmly resolved that she would take charge of her life and see what steps she had to take.

Dev had called sometime back and asked her to get ready to go shopping. He always had 'plans' for them. She did not want to go anywhere; she did not want to do anything. She just loved hanging around home after work. On weekends, she enjoyed watching a movie, preferably in a theatre. She loved the whole experience. He couldn't even sit through a DVD. He loved noise; always wanted to go some place, do something. He sought activity all the time. He would say 'let's go out for dinner or to someone's place or invite someone home.' She would feign headaches or exhaustion and encourage him to go on his own. But now she knew she had no way out -- he had a valid reason to take her shopping. The time had come to shift into the new house, and as was his wont, he had taken charge. He hurried her like usual the moment he arrived and, increased her stress levels for nothing. They were only going shopping for god's sake, not rushing somebody to the hospital! In an hour, Dev had bought her a raw silk sari with a zari border, a diamond and South sea pearl set. She accepted them with an oblique smile. Earlier, she had to make an effort to smile when she knew he expected one. But after so many years, it had become a permanent fixture in her life. She no longer needed to try. How simple submissiveness was, and, yet how heart breaking when you have a mind that thinks... a body that feels... how both feel dead if you don't think or feel. But she had done a good job of it so far. Of pretending to be alive when she was festering from within. As rotten as a dead body that had decayed long ago and nothing was left to show that there was once life in there. But her mind was constantly fantasizing. It hadn't been easy to rein in her mind like she had done with her body.

She lived in her mind most of the time. She imagined her married life with different beginnings but the end was always the same for every story her mind plotted. Liberation from this control. Freedom from domination. Independence. Bliss. Another man. Another place. Heaven. Caring. Understanding. Tenderness. Breathing. Paradise she had never gained. The Hades she was desperate to escape. Even now, as she was making the right noises in response to his stern instructions, her mind was at work. It gave her sadistic pleasure when she imagined what a blow he was about to get. What made it more pleasurable was the fact that she would be the perpetrator, for a change. He would be at the receiving end. This was her one chance. The first and probably the last, if she wanted to lead a normal life of dignity and respect in her own eyes. Right now, she had the dignity in the eyes of the society as the wife of a wealthy businessman. Respect as the mother of two sons. Respectable. But when she looked at the mirror, she only saw a zombie that was going through the motions in the movie called life. This is not me, eating, drinking, working, fornicating... It was eerie to feel so remote.

He had made available to her every luxury money could buy – food, drink, clothes, jewellery, (chosen by him) holidays to exotic destinations (always planned by him). They even had sex when he was 'in the mood'. But that was one area where she had no desire to play a role. She allowed him to take her body whenever he reached for her. Why she did that, she didn't know. One reason could be that it lasted exactly for one or at best two minutes. Before she even felt anything – pleasure or disgust – it was over. Sometimes he didn't even enter her properly but he still went through the whole act with the same pleasure. He thrusted, he heaved, he groaned and he shuddered. That was the beauty of being a woman. You can take it lying down and be done with it.

She had read somewhere that a normal sexual act minus the foreplay took eleven minutes. ELEVEN MINUTES. Sounded like a bloody marathon to her. To the outside world, he appeared to be a tall, well-built, masculine, virile man. Virility, who knew it better than her, had nothing to with performance or the lack of it.

For a woman to get pregnant, having an orgasm was not a prerequisite. Had it been, India wouldn't have to do anything to control its population. Only less then half or quarter or probably none of the women would get pregnant. Nor was it mandatory for a man to feel one with the woman to sow his seed in her. Copulate. Populate. Nothing more. Nothing less.

Thank God she loved her children. At least she had been lucky to experience that emotion. She had been a passionate mother from the time she had conceived. She did everything that was recommended by the doctors, by the books, by friends. She left no advice unheeded to have healthy babies. She wanted a boy desperately both the times. In this one area, her wishes were fulfilled. Both the times she had shuddered with fear at the thought of bearing a daughter. No, no way would she able to endure the transformation of a lively girl into a lifeless robot. She didn't have it in her to raise a daughter. If you had to lead by example, she was a pathetic one. So pathetic that of late, she had begun thinking of ending this whole farce. She was tired of conforming, of following rules, of being shown her place. Oh, she was really tired.

Whenever she saw her sons, she felt guilty for having entertained such criminal thoughts. Once you bring a new life into this world, you cease to have any rights over your own. Sometimes, she wondered why killing oneself was made into such a big deal. You were only killing yourself, not murdering somebody else. If living is a privilege, why couldn't dying be the same? First of all, you have no say in your birth; does that mean you shouldn't have any in your death as well? In the Gita, Krishna said that there is no death for the soul. It's only the body, which dies. Elsewhere, she had read that dying is like shedding your clothes. Then why couldn't you shed them when you wished to? This whole religious funda was meant for the plebeians, looks like. People for whom emotional crutches are needed to retain their equilibrium.

Anyway, that option was closed to her now. She loved her babies too much to do that. But there was something she could do now, if she acted well on time. The opportunity had presented itself so beautifully. Almost custom delivered at her doorstep. There would be no confrontations. No ugly scenes. No verbal duels. No contests. Just one move. In fact, the exit route was perfect. It was HE who would move out to enter HIS dream house. She would tell him on the day of the house warming puja that she had begun her menstrual period. He had always been superstitious about a woman's 'that time of the month.' Part of his feudal upbringing. She always wondered how anybody could believe in such crap. How could the essence of being a woman, the prerequisite for being a mother, be considered impure? But now, she was glad he thought so. Finally she could reclaim her life. Her children could do without the tyrannical influence of their father. The chance of the boys imbibing their father's value system was a strong possibility. Dev was debatably an excellent father. He was proud of the fact that he was a father of boys. The upkeepers of his family tree. That's what made it all the more important to remove them from such mindsets where a mother had practically no role to play. She had brought them into this world. Now it was her duty to ensure they grew up into sensitive human beings. Not just sensitive to how others treat them but also to how they treat others. That was most important. Dev constantly told her that he was a sensitive person. "I get hurt easily when people are inconsiderate." What he meant was he was touchy. If somebody said something he felt was rude, his ego hurt. But that didn't make him any more sensitive to other's feelings about his behaviour. He wasn't just a rude man he was plain arrogant. He thought he was god's gift to mankind. He rode rough shod over others. He had to have his way no matter what. Now, how he could claim to be sensitive, Vaidehi couldn't fathom. In any case, she would soon be free. She knew she had an uneven road ahead but she was ready for the bumps. When you decide on your destination, the path becomes inconsequential. It doesn't matter where you are, what matters is where you plan to reach. That's what gives you peace.

The plan was perfectly carried out with least effort. On the eve of their house-warming day, she broke the news to Dev. Expectedly, he was livid. How could you not remember your dates, he yelled at her. Such an irresponsible, mindless woman he had never met in his life, he told the boys who were clueless. In my mother's house, all the women keep a track of their dates when they have to plan auspicious celebrations, he ranted. "Next time you tell me ma, I'll remember all your dates and remind you," Vedant suggested. He hated it when his father screamed at his mother every now and then. Vaidehi smiled at her son and Dev got even more furious, "Why do you want to drag children into this nonsense?" he screamed his lungs out. That scared Vedant and he hugged her and pressed his head on her waist. She ruffled his hair as if to say she appreciated his support. Dev looked at the two of them and was visibly disturbed. "Say something," he demanded. It got his goat when she didn't react to his outbursts. But she never did.

For Vaidehi, it was easier this time to take it in her stride. One last time was not so difficult. In a few hours, she would be breathing freely. And that was well worth everything, every slight, every hurt. Finally, she would be free. As breeze. She could go whichever way she pleased. Pause at her will. Move at her pace. Now, that would be heaven on this earth. Her idea of one. In this planet. In her world. In her life.

She didn't know what she would do with her freedom. She was not even sure if it would make her happier. All she knew was that her life would be in her possession. At her will. At her command. How else could one reach the destination? Or even plan a route to get to it? Her life with Dev had become a business. Barter. His capital and her investment. Their joint account – their children. Their conversation – more like his – invariably revolved around their joint account. How to nurture it, how to make it grow, what to do with it when it grows, how to handle it on a day-to-day basis. Not once did she agree with his views. But she never felt the need to express her opinions. She knew there was no point. And mostly, she didn't believe in frittering away her energies on futile pursuits. Trying to make him see her point of view was futile. Loads of arguments during their initial years of marriage had taught her that invaluable lesson.

Sometimes she would look at herself in the mirror and wonder who the reflection belonged to. The woman in front of her was a stranger. This image was not her reflection; it was more like a shadow. It led her wherever she went.

Dev was the sunlight that brought out her shadow. Aptly, he behaved like the sun rose from his arse. What a paradox! For a shadow to be present, you need sunshine. Bright, life giving sunlight to bring out the dark shadow of self.

His temper flared up at the slightest opposition to his ideas. No matter who they came from. His parents, his wife or his children. He indulged them no end but there was a catch to it. Obey me people; agree with me, flatter me and I'll pamper you. Simple. Straight. Black and white. No dissence. No gray. Life was hunky dory. When not hunky dory, it was stinky gory. Hunky dory meant gifts and endearments. Stinky gory meant abuses and indifference. He had even struck her a couple of times and accused her after that for provoking him. Everything happened to be her fault. All she had said was that he was increasingly becoming like his father whom he despised from the core of his being. His father, apparently, had hit his mother while he watched on helplessly. "Just imagine. Something snapped in me. After that I felt no affection or respect for my father, ever," he had told her once. Vaidehi thought to herself how he had subconsciously begun to ape the very person he was so irreverent of!

Rukmini Naidu was chatting up Shashikala who had brought a bunch of photographs of eligible girls in the Naidu community with her. "Akka (Sister), this is the right time," she said to Rukmini, "It is the right age for Prabhat. You look at the pictures now. Then you can consult with bava (Brother-in-law). What do you say?"

Rukmini nodded, scanning the pictures at arm's length. She screwed her eyes hoping to get a clearer view. "Why don't you wear your glasses, akka?" Shashi suggested. Rukmini had distaste for spectacles. Yet, she walked in looking for them. After all, it was the question of her son's life. She couldn't afford to be short sighted. She found them lying on the bed side. She polished them with the soft cloth from the case as she walked to the drawing room. Then, she settled down on the sofa. With clearer vision and everything set, she went through the whole bunch with great concentration. Shashi hummed a Telugu song from the latest hit movie to keep her mouth occupied as her friend busied herself with the task on hand. After a while, Rukmini said, "All of them are pretty, Shashi. I can't make up my mind." "That's true akka. Nowadays all girls are so well turned out. Everybody is educating their daughters in the best of universities across the world. With that kind of exposure any girl will turn out well groomed. Look at you and me. We never had such advantages but still we haven't done too badly. What do you say?" Rukmini agreed. Shashi suggested she show the photos to her husband and son and they could take it from there. With the matter out of the way, both the women drank their cups of tea with chudwa and khara boondi, while exchanging trivia about this and that. Rukmini felt at peace now that she had set the ball rolling.

Prabhat was taking his boss, the General Manager (GM), through a PPT presentation that he had put together for an MNC client's impending conference. Vithal was impressed. He walked from his side to where Prabhat was seated. "Good show, Prabhat. I think that's brilliant," he said extending his hand. Prabhat stood up and placed his hand limply in Vithal's firm warm palm. The handshake done, Vithal also gave him a bear hug. Prabhat thought he had died and gone to heaven. It felt so good to be held by the one he was so deeply attracted to. Also, it had been so long since a man had touched him like this. He could feel blood rushing to his vitals and before it could be the cause of his embarrassment, he moved away and mumbled, "Thank you. I'm glad you like it." From that moment on, Prabhat's clamouring for his boss intensified a million times. He wanted more. For some reason, he felt Vithal was drawn to him as well. But how was he going to find out for sure? When he returned to his cabin, he found Sailaja, the front office manager waiting for him. She beamed when he looked at her and thrust some letters that needed the GM's signature. He ordered them each a cup of coffee. They got talking. "How's the boss's mood?" she asked him. Vithal's moods were famous wherever he had worked so far. "Sometimes I think everything depends on which side of the bed he wakes up from in the morning." She continued.

"It's not so bad, Sailaja. Today, especially, he's in a fab mood," he responded.

"Thank goodness," she said, "I need his signatures for many important matters. When can I come back to pick them up?"

"I will buzz you or have it sent across as soon as he signs them."

Their cups of coffee arrived and Sailaja cribbed that it had gotten cold.

"That's because you asked for south Indian coffee. The decoction is normally cold and you need to add real hot milk if you want regular temperature. Here, have mine. I always ask for readymade coffee and check, how hot it is."

"Didn't know that," Sailaja reached for his cup, "Thanks for the tip. Listen, I heard madam has booked a table for twenty for her kitty party lunch.'

"Which madam?"

"GM's wife?"

"So what's the big deal about her kitty party lunch?'

"Have you met her?'

"No, I haven't"

"That explains. She's one big fusspot. Everything has to be just so. Exactly the way she wants. The lime slice in her vodka has to be a perfect round, 1 mm in size, ice cubes perfectly formed, filled to the brim of her glass. If it is wine, measured to precision, pizza has to be thin crust, pasta has to be al dente, uff, she drives the entire kitchen crazy with her demands. The coffee shop manager must be climbing walls already. Just the thought of her lunch must be driving him nuts."

Prabhat felt weird inside. Vithal's wife. What kind of a lover was he? Passionate, sensitive, demanding or selfish?

"Hey, what's the matter? You look lost. Did I say something I shouldn't have about the boss' wife?"

"Oh no, Sailu. Just got distracted. Nothing to do with what you said," he lied.

Sailaja liked Prabhat. He was a caring guy. The kind she liked. But he never ever showed any signs of being interested in her. She left, wondering what kind of women he liked.

Prabhat couldn't concentrate on anything for a long time that day. Vithal having a wife bothered him. contantly. The fact that he had a wife, that he had a love life, the doubt that he may not be open to a different relationship, kept cropping up in his mind. Why would somebody who has experienced the pleasure of sex with a woman be interested otherwise? How could he find out? He should have asked Sailaja. He reached for the phone and dialed her extension. She was sitting in front of him in less than five minutes. They talked about this and that and he asked her, "So when are you getting married Sailu?"

"Not you too Prabhat. I am sick and tired of hearing this question. Why don't you tell me about yourself?'

"Haven't a clue. Don't even want to think about it. How long do you think our boss has been married?"

"Must be 5 years at least. Why?'

"Tell me something. Have you heard anything unusual about him?"

"You mean his swinging both ways? Of course, I have. Your predecessor, Shrikant, asked for a transfer apparently because he couldn't handle our man's overtures."

"Really? Was Shrikant handsome?"

"You surprise me, Prabhat! How does it matter if Shrikant was handsome or not? All you men are strange." Sailaja grumbled.

Prabhat bit his tongue. What the hell was he doing? But, all the questioning had been worth it. At least, he had some hope now. Though he felt envious of Mrs. Boss as well as his predecessor. He turned his attention to the email he was supposed to send. Just then, Vithal walked into his cabin, towards his side of the table. Prabhat stood up to acknowledge his arrival. Both men stood face to face. In an instant, the Vithal reached out for Prabhat's waist. Prabhat could do nothing to conceal his strong desire. When Vithal felt it, he smiled while looking deeply into the younger man's eyes and said, "Why didn't you tell me before what you feel for me?' Prabhat couldn't reply. He seemed to have lost his voice. There was a knock on the door and Vithal sprinted to the other side pretending to look at some file. It was somebody from the housekeeping staff for the daily cleaning ritual. Prabhat told him to come later. Vithal stopped his pretence and said, "Listen, it's quite risky here. Tomorrow, I need to inspect the new rooms on the fifth floor. There will be nobody in there. You can join me if you like." He winked and left.

If he liked? If he could, he would follow him right now. Didn't matter where they went. As long as they could be alone together. Prabhat stood transfixed. His body had turned feverish. His breath felt hot-as-hell. He sat down with a thud on his revolving chair, which moved some distance and smiled to himself. He felt so happy at the turn of events. His body ached now with unfulfilled desire. He sighed at the thought of having to wait till tomorrow.

He drove home in euphoria. He hadn't experienced such intensity before. His last, also his first, affair paled in comparison. He hugged his mother who had come out to receive him when she heard his bike. "What kanna (endearment)? You seem very happy today," she smiled at the sight of his beaming face. She always felt happy when she saw him in a good mood.

"Yes ma. Had a good day at work."

"Found some girl or what? I hope you have. Saves me the trouble of looking for one."

Prabhat didn't reply but was quite impressed with his mother's near accuracy. Had he been a regular man, her observation would have hit the right spot. Bingo.

His mother continued, "You freshen up now. I've made some fresh cheese sandwiches for you and then we can talk. Let me get some coffee."

He hummed as he freshened up, feeling on top of the world. Everything felt extra-nice. His mother's soft sandwiches were delicious. She watched him smugly as he ate. Nothing in this world can beat the pleasure of feeding one's child even if that child has long outgrown childhood. Once she made sure that he had eaten just a bit more than his usual appetite, she placed a steaming mug of filter coffee and said, "Kanna, Shashi aunty was here this afternoon."

"OH NO! Not now ma, please," he pleaded.

"Ok fine. I won't say anything now. I have kept some photos in your room. See them when you feel like. No pressure, ra kanna, just take a look at them, once. Please."

Oh God, he had almost forgotten about all this. He didn't even have the space to relish what he had experienced. The same experience would have been so acceptable had he been a regular guy. In fact, his mother had just said that she welcomed it. If only he had had normal preferences. Life would have been simpler. But now he had no choice but to accept himself the way he was. The possibility of others around him accepting his different choice was rather remote, closer to impossibility. There was no point trying. First things first, he had to put off his mother's plans. He could deal with other things later.

He walked into his room and when he reached for the TV remote that was lying on his bedside, he found a photo album. He chucked the remote and browsed through the pictures. Most of them were young and attractive. For a second, he felt really bad for them. Imagine being exhibited this way in the name of a marriage alliance. Even a guy like him who wasn't the least bit interested in them, had access to their personal details. Why would smart girls like these agree for something so whore-like, he wondered, when it came to one of the most important relationships in human life? Rukmini Devi who had stepped into his door stopped herself when she found him looking intently at the photos. For all that drama, she smiled to herself, looked like her son was quite interested. She hoped at least one girl would do it. Truth is not what we see, but the way we perceive what we see. She hadn't a clue that she was farthest from her son's truth. Her extreme love for him was blinding her to reality. That's what happens in most close relationships. We see what we wish to see. Sometimes, imagining things that don't exist and remaining oblivious to those that do. Most of our comforts and discomforts arise from our perceived realities.

Rishi was winding things up at the office so that he could take a break for a couple of hours. Just when he was about to leave, Priyamvada walked in. He exchanged pleasantries and as he was telling her that he was in a hurry his cell phone rang. The moment he looked at the number, his stress levels went up. "Give me five minutes, just five minutes, I'm on my way," he said and rushed out without bothering to say bye to Priyamvada.

Rishi stepped on the gas, driving rasher than necessary. Why did it always turn out this way, he wondered. Every other appointment, he always made it on time. But when it came to her, for some reason, he was always late. He couldn't blame her for getting annoyed with him. She had specifically told him when they had met the last time that she could spend just an hour with him and to not to be late. Now she must be fuming while waiting for him. Good, he had the foresight to give her the spare key. At least, she didn't have to hang around outside. He parked his car in his lot and rushed to his first floor apartment climbing two steps at a time. He stood huffing as he rang the bell. She opened the door in a split second as if she was waiting on the other side of the door and surprise of surprises, smiled at him. Menaka actually smiled at Rishi. And here he was ready with all his excuses. She just grabbed him in, pinned him against the door, and crushed her lips against his mumbling, "Bastard, you haven't changed!" He wanted to say something appropriate but didn't know what to say that wouldn't spoil it for him. For her, actually. He preferred returning her favour by grabbing her around the waist even harder and dragging her to the sofa. The same one that she used to sit on and watch TV a few years ago.

They lay there talking when they were spent. He said to her, "You know I was so scared when I was late again today."

She laughed as if she derived some sadistic pleasure and said, "Lucky you! I had decided to wait precisely for fifteen minutes and leave."

"But if this is how your response is, I don't mind repeating it."

"Oh well, I knew I had only an hour with you. Sulking would have been such a waste of time, you see."

"Like that? You're so unpredictable you know that, don't you Minnie? But your logic is brilliant."

"Yeah, right! Seriously, why don't you just start a little earlier considering the traffic is so chaotic these days? Look at me; I reached here after a half hour drive. And your office is on the next street. I can never understand why you do this to me again and again."

"Shucks, why did I have to start this? I need to kick myself. Now you'll be all upset and irritated."

She felt sorry when he said that. She ruffled his hair and said with a smile, "No baby, nevvver. I will never get upset with you now. But you should also try to change your ways, Rishi."

"I promise."

"You keep promising all the time. And then you break them consistently."

"Promises are like pie crusts baby. The fun is in breaking 'em. But wait, I can't afford it now. Not after the lesson you've taught me, my dear Minnie," he said kissing her on the lips. She responded for a while and resisted suddenly.

"What's the matter?" he asked.

"I got to go, Rishi. Dev has turned very suspicious these days. He keeps track of all my movements. It's so irritating."

Just the mention of his name irked Rishi.

"So what if he's suspicious? It's working. Don't you see that? And I had no clue what you were doing in my absence because I trusted you so much."

"It had nothing to do with your trust. You were plain disinterested in me. Dev is crazy about me. That's what makes him possessive."

"Oh yeah? So what are you doing with a wimp like me when you have a possessive husband waiting for you at home?'

"I am an idiot. A prime ass. I have no idea what I'm doing here."

"Oh, please. You know exactly why you're here. It's me who's an ass. Allowing myself to be used and dumped and reused."

"What the hell do you mean by being used? In what way am I using you? I walked out of the house. I took nothing from you. Even now, I don't need your money."

"Who's talking about money? Being used is not only about that. You are exploiting my feelings for you."

"Am I? Your spending an hour with me is exploitation? God knows what you mean. Anyway, I have no time for arguments now. Just a while ago, you said you wouldn't be unreasonable. And now this! You'll never change, Rishi. I don't know why I keep expecting you to understand me."

She left without saying bye to him. What made him react like that, he wondered. He was by no means the possessive sort. In fact, he believed in total freedom within a relationship. Probably, that had been his undoing in his marriage. But he was not about to change his belief system now. He had to make up with her now. The urgency was so strong that he reached for his phone and called her on hers. She sounded distant. "Listen, Minnie, I'm sorry for whatever I said." She didn't respond. "Are you listening?" he asked. That's when he heard her sobbing. He felt like such a heel for hurting her. "Minnie, please come back now, I am really sorry. I have no idea what I was saying. Guess I am so miserable without you that I blurted out nonsense."

She replied finally, "No, Rishi. It's okay. I deserve this for what I did to you.'

"Can we meet now?"

"Not now. I'll see you tomorrow. I will come home during lunch hour. Bye for now."

He hung up and realized that Menaka hadn't changed one bit. One moment she would be spitting fire and the next she would cry like a wounded child. Either way, she made him feel lousy.

He lay there feeling abandoned and lonely. Surveying the emptiness of the apartment, he wondered how just one woman was enough to fill that space. Just one more person and his house had been alive. His life had been full. Before he could succumb to self pity, he freshened up and got back to work. He would work like a maniac for the rest of the day until it was dark and he was hungry or tired.

When he was a married man, he used to work because the work was demanding, much as he wanted to get home to the woman who waited for him, now he created work even when there was not much because he couldn't bear the vacuum that was left by the same woman.

Priyamvada dropped in again to see him at the end of the day. He smiled and she said, "Not bad. Somebody is in a good mood today."

He smiled some more and she continued, "I'm so bored today. Why don't we go out for a drink?" He agreed and they headed out to a new resto-bar that had opened recently. He relaxed as the first drink went in and settled down comfortably. She was interesting company and she made him laugh quite a bit with her mimicking of their clients and other colleagues. More than anything, she made him feel good. She was openly appreciative of his wit, which boosted his flagging sense of humour and morale. She made no mention of the earlier fiasco. A step further, she invited him into her house again when he went to drop her. He looked at his watch. It wasn't too late. He needed to take his mind off Menaka. So he agreed and followed her in. Unsurprisingly, he thought of Menaka and what they had done earlier in the day. That's when Priyamvada moved closer to him and put his arms around her waist. She circled hers around his neck and looked at him gingerly. By then the effect of alcohol and his memories had warmed him enough to her and they kissed. His body responded wonderfully and as they moved in rhythm, Priya sighed, satiated and relieved that she was not so undesirable, after all.

He reached home, kicked off his shoes and crashed in an instant with his clothes and socks on. After years, sleep had chosen him that night. Tomorrow would be another day…

Chapter X

Dev was most upset during the Griha Pravesh Puja (House warming ceremony). His wife was a total dunce. How could she be so forgetful? Anyway, his sons were with him and that more than made up for her absence. The ceremony went off well but the guests kept enquiring about his wife. The boys loved the house. He had taken special care with the décor of their rooms. It was decided, actually he had decided that the boys would share one room until Karan was old enough for a room of his own. He told Vedant, "You can do whatever you want. Put up posters of your favourite bikes, cars, rock stars, whatever. But no girls, ok?" All three of them laughed. The boys loved their dad. He always gave them everything they wanted even before they asked. And if they did have a special request he would move heaven and earth to fulfill it. But they loved their mother a little more. Her warmth was something else.

After the guests left, Karan wanted his mom. Dev's irritation returned. The priest had told him that the house should not be left uninhabited after the ceremony. At least one of them had to sleep for three consecutive nights under the new roof. He had no choice but to drop them back to their old house, to their mother. Had everything else been in place, he could have somehow cajoled them to stay back. Plus they also had school to attend the next day.

When he dropped them back, he felt that Vaidehi seemed switched off. Though she did enquire, "How did everything go?" It sounded more like courtesy than involvement. "Went off really well. Everybody was asking where you were." She didn't say a word. He asked her, "What's for dinner?"

"Don't you have to go back to the new house?" she asked as if she dreaded the prospect of him staying back.

"Why don't you answer my question? You're so annoying, I tell you. Of course, I have to. Don't I have the right to know?"

Where did the question of rights and privileges arise, she wondered?

"The usual fare. Lakshmi has made tomato dal, gobi, rasam, and rice. You want to eat?"

"Oh no. I'm not hungry. I have packed some pulihora and prasadam for you." He said and walked into their bedroom. He removed a rucksack, threw in some clothes from his closet, kissed the boys good night and left. It felt vague, leaving his home, the house where they had lived for so long, where his sons had been born. If this idiotic woman had planned things properly, they could have been together in the new house. He threw an angry look at her and left. Vaidehi wondered, now what?

As soon as he left, she perked up. She held her sons close and swung them around, "Badmash bachchas, you didn't miss mommy?" The house resonated with their laughter. And then, she said, "I am going to feed you today." They welcomed her suggestion amidst peals of laughter. She felt content as she fed them spoonfuls of dal rice in turns. Dev always screamed at her when she did that in his presence. "Let them be independent!" he would thunder, "Don't turn them into sissies!" She celebrated the first night of her freedom by doing what pleased her the most. She was taken aback when he had enquired about dinner. What if he decided to stay back? Thank God, he hadn't. She hugged her sons to her bosom and planted kisses on their heads. Lakshmi looked at them and thought how secure children feel in their mother's embrace. Little did she know that it was Vaidehi who was deriving security from their presence; it was she who lapped up comfort from the embrace.

Ever since Vedant was born, she could sleep in the nights only when he was next to her on the same bed. She would open his teeny weenie fist and place her finger, which he would promptly clutch, until she drifted off to sleep. And after Karan joined the family, she would take turns and put her arms around them. For her, her sons were her life, the fulcrum of her existence. She couldn't remember her married life before they arrived.

"Amma (Madam), do you need anything? I have kept water next to your bed."
Lakshmi said. Vaidehi thanked her and told her to sleep. "Mummy, when will
we move to our new house?' Vedant wanted to know, "It's very nice. My room
is so big," he said widening his arms. She evaded and said, "Let's sleep baby. I'm
tired." In a jiffy he was asleep. She spent the rest of the night looking at her sons
and thinking. What would she tell them? Obviously, they needed to know that
she had no intentions of moving into the new house. Was she doing the right
thing? Was she jeopardizing their future for selfish reasons? She thought of Dev
and she knew she had no choice. She had had enough of his domineering ways.
She had no future with him. She never missed his presence. In fact, his absence
was liberating. She tried remembering happy phases of their relationship. None
came to her mind. Except the ones they shared with their children. As parents,
they had a bond but as life mates they had nothing going for them. Did they
ever share any chemistry? They had, probably, but the memory was so distant
that it had faded.

Two streets away, Dev was wide-awake. He had had his two customary drinks
with a couple of his buddies. When they left, he was surrounded by silence.
He didn't know what to do. He switched on the TV. The cable connection was
not in place but doordarshan was on. Some vague looking dancer was prancing
around in the name of classical dance to the tune of a screechy carnatic singer.
That stupid wife of his loved classical music, both carnatic and Hindustani. He
knew it upset her whenever he made fun of it. He flipped the channel only to
catch a tribal dance on DD metro. He felt far removed from life as he looked
at the semi clad adivasis gyrating to their own rhythm.

It had been years since he had been alone, on his own, like this. Probably,
never. His parents's home always had people. And then there was Vaidehi. A
little later, their sons. He smiled when he thought of them. He adored them.
Every evening as soon as he reached home from work, he would wash up and
all of them would have something to eat. The boys would have their sandwiches
and milk, they their cups of tea with biscuits or some savory stuff. The house
would be filled with noise and activity. And then, the boys and he would head
out to the garden and play football or cricket till it was dark or the tuition
master arrived, whichever happened first. Then the boys would get busy with
their studies. He would watch news till it was dinnertime. They would gather
at the dining table and create such a ruckus while eating. It wasn't even a few
hours and he was missing them terribly. Every little detail, every memory,
every normal occurrence seemed magnified, larger than life. Dev realized that

night that he had no life without his family. If he could see into the future, he would probably have foreseen that his life, the way he wanted it, had ended that very night.

If he had guessed it even once, if the thought had crossed his mind even in his wildest dream, Dev wouldn't have been as shocked as he turned out to be when his wife showed no signs of moving into their new home. He had decided earlier that the new house would have new furniture since the stuff they owned was too old. After spending three nights on his own, he asked her to accompany him to the interior designer who would do up their new home. She said she wasn't interested and that he could make the decision on his own.

"I will come and fetch you from your office and then we will meet Arpita Khan, the designer. She's excellent. I have seen her work. Very impressive," he said.

"Why don't you do it on your own?" she replied.

"I don't believe this. You don't sound enthusiastic at all about our new home.'

"Like always, you're right."

"What do you mean by that?"

"I am not interested in your new house?"

"Why?'

"Because I have no intentions of moving in there."

"How come you never told me that before?"

"You never asked me, that's why."

"Let me make one thing clear to you, Vaidehi. I am not going to come back to the old house."

"Thank God. If you do, I'll move out from there too."

"What are you saying?"

"I want to separate, that's what I'm saying."

By then Dev had lost it. He drove like a maniac and reached her house, their old home, but she wasn't in. Nor were the boys. Lakshmi informed him that they had gone to watch a movie. Dev hated watching movies and hated it even more when she went for one. He decided to wait. Suddenly, the house didn't feel like his after Vaidehi had told in no uncertain terms that she didn't want to be with him anymore. What was going on, really? Should he ask her to rethink what she was suggesting? Why should he? It wasn't his fault. Moreover, he had pampered her enough. Let her experience life a bit. That should straighten her out. He decided to withdraw all the money from their joint account and leave the minimum balance. He had to teach her a lesson. High time. He had spoiled her enough. And yes, he would take his sons away with him once everything was in place in the house. She will come begging on her knees. He had to control himself from thrashing her because his blood was boiling. If she hadn't been the mother of his sons he would have shown her her place. He waited for three hours and still there were no signs. He didn't feel like going into their bedroom after she had shut him out so rudely. So he sat in the living room flicking channels on the TV. Nothing held his attention. He paced up and down. Finally, Lakshmi asked him if he would like to eat dinner. "I'll wait for Karan and Vedant," he replied.

"Saar, but amma said they would eat outside and come."

"Why didn't you tell me before?' He screamed and walked out. He didn't know where to go. After driving aimlessly for sometime, he decided to visit his friend, Ashfaq.

Ashfaq and he had grown up together. Studied in the same school, same college, sometimes dated the same girl, one after another, of course, and knew everything about each other. When Ashfaq saw him, he asked, "What's the matter, yaar? Why are you looking like your wife has run away with somebody?"

"Stop joking, Ashfaq. Vaidehi's been acting funny. Says she wants to separate."

"Asshole, what did you do? Did you scream at her? Did you have a fight?'

Dev shared with him the sequence of events. Ashfaq listened quietly. Much as he loved his friend, he knew there was more to it. Why would a woman after having two children want out? He had met Vaidehi a number of times and she seemed like a peaceful person. But Dev was unable to put a finger on it. After discussing the issue for a while, Ashfaq said, "Let me try. I will talk to Vaidehi tomorrow and find out what exactly is going on in her mind. Why don't you stay back tonight with me? Hajera has gone to Canada with the kids to look up her uncle, anyway. I am the king of the house for another week. Let's have a drink."

Ashfaq brought out black label to distract his friend's mind from what was brewing in there. They drank till late night. Ashfaq lived life king size mostly since his ancestral properties ran into billions though between his five brothers and himself, they had managed to wipe quite a few clean. Now, the property had been divided with each son getting his due share. This house he lived in was a part of his inheritance. Luckily, he had struck gold recently with the boom in the share market. Plus his father-in-law who happened to own a leather factory had died recently bequeathing everything to his only daughter. That had made Ashfaq's wife, Hajera wealthier than him. She neither asked him for money nor gave him any. But they were happy. Very few relationships worked so well when there was no exchange of the material sort. They had met in Nizam's college when they were students. In fact, all of them were part of the same group. Dev was quite fond of Hajera too. Very few people who knew her, were not fond of her. In addition to being breathtakingly beautiful, Hajera was a good soul and it shone through. She loved people and people loved her. She loved the whole deal about cooking, hosting, giving and life in general. Ashfaq complemented her totally. He was as good looking if not better, tall, well built, brown hair, as fair skinned as an Indian can get, gray eyes and a regal aura. They looked every inch a royal couple. During the initial years of their respective marriages and before the children made their appearance, the four of them hung out together a great deal. In fact Hajera was one of the few women Vaidehi was fond of. Of late, they had sort of drifted apart because Dev and Vaidehi had gotten very busy with their careers and children.

The next morning when Dev opened his eyes, it was nearing noon. He hadn't slept this late in a long time. He picked up his cell phone and realized it was dead. He had forgotten to carry his charger so he walked to the landline in the living room and rung his office. He informed his manager that he was unwell. Before turning in, he had decided that he'd drop his sons to school and then find out what exactly Vaidehi wanted. But now, it was too late. In a while it would be lunch break for the boys. Vaidehi would be neck deep in work. Anyway, he had the whole day to himself. He could plan his move in leisure. When he walked out after a bath, he found Ashfaq lounging in the verandah poring over the newspapers. There were half a dozen newspapers strewn around him. When he saw Dev, he stretched himself yawning and called out to the servant, "Ruksana bee, tea, toast and biscuits for saab, quick." Dev was apologetic about waking up late.

"Don't behave like a stranger, you fool," Ashfaq said, "This is my normal wake up time."

They chatted about the rise and fall of the stock market, inconsistency of Indian cricketers, the new Rolex model and their children's antics. That's when they decided that they would visit Vaidehi in the evening together. It would probably neutralize her mood. For all you know, Ashfaq told his friend, she was just upset over some insensitive remark he had made.

"We men are such bastards, I tell you. We bloody well know that our lives are meaningless without our women and yet we go around trampling on their feelings mercilessly. The worst part is we are not even aware of what we're doing. Remember Ballu, the bear. That sard yaar, Balwinder Singh, who was with us in college?" Dev nodded in recognition. "I met him the other day," Ashfaq continued, "Poor fellow is divorced. After a couple of drinks he confessed there is nothing like being married. Now he's having hazaar flings. But he says there's no lasting satisfaction in it. Always yearning, craving, wanting company. Time for you to wake up, my dear friend. Understand where you have gone wrong. Don't know why but I am feeling dreadfully lazy today."

"Tell me something new, Ashfaq."

Dev stayed pensive the whole day. While they were eating lunch, Ashfaq remarked, "You know what bugger, I think you're too stuck up about everything. You need to loosen up a bit. Be less of a control freak."

"Stop lecturing now, Ashfaq. Just because I am at your mercy, don't think you can say what you want. I didn't get everything on a platter like you did."

"Except a million rupees from your father as investment."

"What's a million compared to your billions? And don't forget I have built a whole empire with that million and returned the money to my father. So, you see, mine was a loan from my father not an inheritance."

"Point noted sir. Gustaqi maaf (I beg your pardon)," Ashfaq laughed.

Later in the day, they got out for their collective mission. On the way Ashfaq advised him again, "Don't behave like a pompous ass, now. Vaidehi's an amenable girl. Please don't lose your temper if she says something. You have no idea how Haji and I fight. She lets me have it whenever she thinks I have done something wrong. And let me tell you, more often than not, she's right. These days I accept my mistake when I recognize one. Earlier I wouldn't admit and we would carry on the fight for days. Not worth it, buddy. Not one bit."

The boys came running when they saw their dad. "Papa, you came yesterday?" Karan enquired.

Dev picked him up and gave him a tight kiss on the cheek and replied, "I came to take you out for an ice cream. Where did you people go?"

"Papa, we went to see Shrek 2. It was so much fun. Then mummy took us for dinner and we had ice cream also. I had two, two."

"You should have had three, three, no," Dev teased him. Vedant went on to narrate his own version. Dev was ecstatic. How much he had missed them! He just had to have them back. Just then Vaidehi emerged. She looked radiant in a T-shirt and jeans. He had seen her in such clothes only before marriage. She looked younger and fresher. Not a trace of worry on her face. She greeted Ashfaq and they hugged. Then she sat down in front of them. Boys ran to her to show off the toys and Toblerone bars that Ashfaq uncle had given them. "So many chocolates, Ashfaq," Vaidehi exclaimed, "What will happen to their teeth?"

"This is the problem with you mothers. You are so paranoid. Haji is also the same. It's okay yaar, once in a while. If you're so concerned, get them to brush their teeth later."

"Yeah, right! That's the easiest task on earth, isn't it?"

They chatted easily. Dev sat quietly conversing with his sons on and off. The tuition master arrived and the boys went into the study. They sat in awkward silence for a bit and then Ashfaq said, "Listen Vaidehi. Please don't misunderstand me. I love you both. I want you both to be happy. Yes, I want to see you two together for the rest of my life. Dev is completely clueless about the problem. He hasn't the faintest idea why you want to separate. I think you should talk and sort out your differences."

Vaidehi looked at Dev who sat like an onlooker. As though he had nothing to do with this conversation. He didn't even look at her. What kind of a conversation can you have with a man who had to depend on his friend to communicate with his wife? How could one sort out differences when there was nothing else in the first place? How could you talk to a person who either screamed or clammed up? She stared at him for a couple of seconds but he was looking everywhere except at her and said, "Ashfaq, this has to be your idea. To me, it seems like he is not one bit interested in talking about anything leave alone our problems. Do you want to know what he did yesterday? He came here when we had gone out for a movie and yelled at Lakshmi. Give me one good reason why anybody would do that. That too because she asked him if he wanted to have dinner."

"Oh, that's what the bitch told you, huh. I'll set her right. Lakshmi, Lakshmi," Dev began yelling.

"Lower your voice Dev," Vaidehi said firmly, "Kids are studying and I will not let you use that language on people who work for us."

"I know. That bitch is more important to you than I am. You trust her more than I do."

"Yes. I trust her and she is important to me because she looks after my house and my kids. And I told you not to speak that way about people who work for us."

"Let's go Ashfaq. After hearing that a bloody servant is more important in this house, I have nothing to talk to her," He said and walked out. Ashfaq didn't know what hit him. He looked at Vaidehi who seemed calm and in control; then he looked at his friend who was already sitting in the car waiting to leave.

Ashfaq said bye to her and sprinted to the car. As soon as he got in, Dev revved up the car noisily. "What was that?" he said to Dev, "We were nowhere near the point and you just took off."

"Forget it," said Dev, "She has always been unreasonable."

"I don't know about the other times but this time, it was you who was unreasonable. Let me tell you."

"Did you see her behavior? The way she was talking? How can you talk to a woman who says she trusts a servant more than me?"

"Really, Dev. I am shocked with your attitude. And I happen to be your closest childhood friend."

Dev didn't respond. There was no point in carrying on the conversation because his friend had no idea about Vaidehi. What Dev conveniently forgot or preferred to, was the fact he was as clueless where she was concerned. He had never tried to interpret her silences and stifled her speech unfailingly.

The next thing he was left dealing with when he returned home after work a few days after was a divorce notice from her. He wasn't in the least bit interested to talk to her. She made no sense anyway. He withdrew all the money from their joint account and filed a petition claiming custody of their kids. Every evening he would go over to 'Vaidehi's house' and wait for the boys to get home from school. The idea was to hassle her, intimidate her with his presence. But she remained stoic. She would speak in a civil tone that one uses with acquaintances, which pissed him off no end. Every time he raised his voice to say something nasty, she would not react. He was at his wit's end.

One evening she returned home and found him playing cricket with the boys in the garden. That was the day for the first time ever, she reacted. She had said, "Dev, I think you should stop coming here in my absence every evening." That was it. He just let it all come out. "You bloody bitch! Who are you to stop me from meeting my sons? I have been putting up with your nonsense but that doesn't mean I am a hijra (eunuch). I am not wearing bangles to dance to your tunes. I will do whatever I want to. Try stopping me!" he growled menacingly. Vaidehi was speechless. She stood there rooted to the ground as the boys dropped their bats and came running to her. They hugged her legs and cried out loudly trying to grapple with the situation. Dev tried pulling them away but they wouldn't let go of the mother and their cries spread across the open air. The elder one, Vedant spoke even as he cried, "Papa, I hate you. I don't want to come with you. You're a horrible man!" Dev let go of his hold on them and slapped her across her face. With tears rolling down her cheeks, she held his palm and spoke in an uneven but firm tone, "Dev, if you don't leave right now, I will call the cops." He could see that she meant it. More than her wrath, public scandal that may ensue terrified him. That was the last time he visited that house. But for several days and nights he couldn't get over his sons' high pitched cries and the hatred in his elder son's eyes. He couldn't bring himself to face them for several days after that.

Over the next few months, the divorce was granted, she had the custody of the kids and he had an absentee parent's status and rights. And like only kids are capable of, they forgot and forgave him at least consciously.

Chapter XI

Love walks into your life, when you're making other plans…

Menaka had walked into his life, when he wasn't even thinking about love, leave alone looking for it. He had had a brief fling with the interior designer of his new house, but had chickened out when she started behaving like they were a couple. He was on the verge of joining the brigade of lonely, husbands-turned-single, desperate, middle aged men when he had noticed her like a bright star on a moonless night. He had gone to one of those staid birthday parties of an acquaintance because he didn't have anything else to do. Nowadays that's all he did anyway. Either he went out to a pub or a party with a bunch of divorced, aimless men like him. He liked to think that he was living it up but every morning when he woke up, he felt like a debauched man. Drinking till midnight and waking up the next noon only to wait for the sun to set when he could hit the bottle again. How he hated this life! Ever since he could remember, he had always pictured himself as a man with a calendar perfect family. Luckily, it had come true. He had married a smart, intelligent woman who'd produced good-looking, bright boys. His heart ached when he thought of his sons. He wouldn't have been devastated had Vaidehi decided to part with him. What shattered him was his boys' absence. His inability to be with them when they were growing up, his helplessness over the legal procedures, his utter failure at having lost his dream was what had destroyed him. He just didn't care any more. His only concern was to get through the day somehow. Without alcohol he would have been a dead man by now. Drugged himself forever with pills or some such drastic thing to sleep and not having to wake up ever again. His dream house had turned out to be a mere shelter. He hated getting back to a home that didn't house his children. That's why his presence at every other party in town was a given. He had become a permanent fixture at parties though he carefully avoided weddings and anniversary parties. Now, at this birthday party, he was bored out of his skull.

The ambience was great, soulful melodies in the background, enough pretty women strutting around, everything was the way it should be at a good party and yet he was listless. He was listening to the whining of his tight fisted, loud-mouthed buddy who had recently been dumped by his wife for a younger man when his eyes travelled to the trio entering the party. That's when he saw this long- haired, fair-complexioned, doe-eyed woman probably in her mid thirties laughing and tilting her head slightly to say something to the woman next to her. He recognized the other woman Leena instantly. His mood lifted immediately when he realized how easy it would be to get an intro to his object of interest. Long since he had seen someone so vibrant, so full of life. He kept observing them and noticed that she laughed a lot, had no qualms about walking up to the bar to ask for a drink, generally didn't give a damn about the people or the party around her. He felt a deep sense of attraction after eons. Finally, he walked up to Leena and said 'Hi.' She looked at him and screamed, "God, Dev, is that you? Of course, what am I asking? You have changed beyond recognition. What have you done to yourself?"

"Just happy being fat."

"Fat, that's an understatement. You are obese."

'You don't have to rub it in, woman."

"Where IS Vaidehi?'

"We split ages ago. Been 6-7 years now.'

"Oh no! I thought you were happy together."

"I thought so too. Only she didn't."

"I am sorry."

"So am I. Now, can we talk about interesting things please? Won't you introduce me to your friends?"

"Sure. Menaka and Sandhya."

They exchanged greetings and when he extended his hand, Menaka said, "Sorry, some other time," pointing to her drink in one hand and flowers in the other.

Dev said, "why don't you give the flowers to whoever they are meant for?"

"Oh, I don't even know the guy. I am yet to meet him. I am a gate crasher basically. In fact, I had forgotten why we're here."

Dev laughed heartily when Leena explained that she had had dragged her to the party despite Menaka's protests. He liked the ease with which Menaka spoke.

Soon they were at his house, the four of them, continuing their drinking session. That's how it had begun – their association – over alcohol and tripe. That night when she got home, unusually Rishi was waiting for her reading in his bed. She had apologized for getting home so late and hit the bed soon after changing. It was already 2 in the morning when she turned off the bed light. She drifted off to sleep in no time. She woke up when somebody tapped her on the arm repeatedly. When she opened her eyes, she saw the form standing next to her bedside. She sat up with a jolt and looked for Rishi next to her. The bed was empty! And the form said, "You're looking for Rishi? He has gone. Very far away from you. To a place that you don't know or recognise. I told you to leave him but you didn't. Now he has gone! What will you do now Menaka? That man you met today, Dev, he has got money. And he's clearly attracted to you. You should go with him. You always wanted to have an easy life, didn't you? In which a man looks after all your needs. Dev will. He's the kind who looks after women. Can't you see? Anyway, now that Rishi has gone very far away from you, do you have a choice? If you don't act quickly, you'll live a life of poverty. Look at yourself. Look, look," the form kept pointing a hazy finger at her body. When she looked at herself, she was shocked. Her clothes were in tatters, exposing one of her breasts, she had bleeding wounds on her arms. She screamed out loud. Somebody was shaking her and she opened her eyes. An alarmed Rishi was asking her, "What happened? Are you okay?" Oh damn! The nightmare had returned. Rishi repeated, "What happened?" She wanted to share it with him but stopped herself. He would just brush it off anyway like he had earlier. Rishi switched on his bed lamp, poured water from the jug next to it into a glass and gave it to her. "Here, drink this." She gulped down the water and her eyes fell on the clock on his side. It was 5 AM! What the hell! What was that dream! She got off the bed and headed to the bathroom.

Routine took over and both of them left to their respective offices. Around noon, the receptionist connected the call from Dev. "Hey," she responded, "How come!" Dev's voice on the phone chuckled and replied, "Normally, people say hi, how are you?" She responded, "Who said I'm normal?" He replied, "So what does an abnormal person like you do in the evenings?" She said, "Well, depends." "How about catching up for a drink tonight? I can pick you up," he suggested. "I'm sure you can. But I am not sure if I want to be," she responded meaning every word. "Why, may I ask," he was not going to give up that easily. "For one, I happen to be married and more importantly, I don't go out with strangers," she explained. "Hmmm," he hesitated and then said, "Just in case you are bored sometime and don't know where to go and if you don't mind giving a stranger an opportunity to become your friend, do call me. Bye for now," he said. She hung up without bothering to say bye.

A month later, after spending a few evenings post work alone at home as Rishi was travelling for a week, she was contemplating on what to do; the TV soaps were getting monotonous and the news channels yawn-worthy. She thought of Dev. Then it occurred to her that she didn't have his number. The only person who could have it was Leena, who had introduced them. Just as she was wondering what she would say, her cell phone rang. It was an unknown number but she ran and answered it, "Hello," she said catching her breath. After a pause a male voice said, "Hi, how are you?" She knew the voice but couldn't put a face to it. "Who's this," she asked. "Stranger who wants to be your friend," he replied. "Oh Dev," she said wondering if he had sixth sense. "Yes ma'am," he replied lightheartedly and continued without much ado, "I have been thinking about you. Would you like to catch up? I can pick you up now if you're free. I am just sitting at home with nothing much to do except watching boring TV." She felt she was hearing her own story from the person she was thinking of reaching out to, so she said yes. That's how it all began as a married woman's distraction from a mundane life.

How or when it had turned serious, Menaka hadn't a clue. All she could remember was that at some point he had begun to fetch her from her office every evening. He would drive her to his house where the two of them would talk for hours over vodka and whisky. Initially, her driver would follow them and she would get back home in her car. After a drink or two she would feel terribly depressed and start blurting out every intimate detail when he would express concern. Soon he was convincing her to leave Rishi and move in with him. At first, she was appalled that he could suggest something so blasphemous. But every evening when she got home and Rishi did something to annoy her, Dev's idea sounded more and more appealing. From appalling to appealing, the change in her response was gradual but consistent. When the opportune moment appeared, she made her exit. Initially, her intention was to teach Rishi a lesson but when he didn't bother to call her or attempt to meet her even once, her meek intention turned into strong resolution – Never to get back to the man who seemed beyond caring. Every evening she cried over his indifference much to Dev's delight. And he made sure he comforted her, reassured her, made her feel special and slowly, steadily warmed his way into the vacuum that she was experiencing. That was the beginning of the end of her relationship with Rishi, in Menaka's mind. Several times she wondered, much later of course, how she could have been such a traitor. Where had her value system gone? Disappeared. Into nothingness. Just because she found an alternative was it fair to let down somebody with whom she had vowed to spend the rest of her life? As long as everything was going according to her idea of a marriage she was fine with Rishi, wasn't she? In health and wealth, yes. In sickness and problems, NO. THAT WAS HER. THAT WAS MENAKA. A woman who bore no resemblance to her when she began life. When had she turned into someone she didn't know and wished she never did? When life throws one of its curves, your real character shines through, her dad had told her when she didn't understand. But when her life sprang a few nasty surprises, her real character crumbled. Or is this her real character? A FAIR WEATHER FRIEND. Probably not. Probably. She wasn't sure of herself any more. One thing she was sure of though – if she hadn't met Dev, she would have still been with Rishi. An avalanche of tears drowned her in their intensity. She sobbed and sobbed until hiccups broke the rhythm of her sobs. She felt miserable. If only she hadn't taken this drastic step! She rued the night she had attended that silly party.

But as far as Dev was concerned, he had fallen in love when he was not even thinking of it. Love had walked into his life, when he was least expecting it…

Chapter XII

When you don't communicate what you feel to your close ones, chances are you alienate them for life

Rukmini was drying her hair in the afternoon sun in her courtyard. A fragrant smoke emanated from the earthenware that contained sambrani on ember. The maidservant held it under her hair with one hand and the other held the edge of Rukmini's hairline. Her eyes closed in involuntarily as she inhaled the fragrance deeply, thoroughly enjoying the sensation. She loved everything about afternoons. She had the whole house to herself. Today, her kitchen was abuzz with avakaya preparations. She had gone with her husband yesterday and bought raw mangoes for the purpose. Veeranna, the mango cutter had arrived an hour ago with his kathipeeta – a mobile knife hinged to a piece of wood. A single mango went under the knife atop the wooden board. Chak, chak, chak went the knife and the result was eight uniform pieces from one mango.

Rukmini's avakaya was legendary. She had turned it into a tradition and carried it out religiously year after year. She picked the ingredients with utmost care - the dry red chillies, mustard seeds, sesame oil, garlic pods. The entire family and the huge circle of their friends awaited eagerly to receive their share every summer. Earlier, she used to send them enough to last the full year but of late, everything had become scarce and expensive. The jadi (ceramic jar) was replaced by emptied bournvita pet bottles.

Two women – Manga and Andal pounded dry red chillies in a stone container with wooden poles. They laughed and chatted as their hands moved in perfect rhythm. One up and one down. The coarse powder wafted in the air and reached Rukmini's nostrils. She sneezed with absolute satisfaction. Good, the chillies had the necessary sting. Her hair had dried now. The maid servant moved away to mind other chores. Rukmini held the edges of her long tresses and inhaled. She loved the smell of sambrani. She always washed her hair with ritha seeds. No shampoos for her. She believed her hair was still long and strong because of her consistent hair care rituals. Her daughter had inherited her hair but she had spoiled it all with shampoos and weird hair colours. And that darned hair dryer she used everyday had damaged her hair so much that now it resembled a coriander bunch.

Rukmini diverted her attention to the present and looked at the mango pieces. She bit into a piece and winked at the sourness. She checked the pounded chilli powder. She always used special chillies and raw sesame oil. Raw preserved the rich red colour and ensured longevity. "Amma, will you mix it now," Andal enquired. She liked this girl Andal. She had come from Tamil Nadu after her husband had abandoned her. Her maali had brought her. Rukmini had taken an instant liking to the timid girl. That was six years ago. Now, nothing in the kitchen moved without her involvement. She had brought in with her the expertise of Tamilian cuisine. With absolute glee Rukmini went about mixing the contents. Satisfied finally, she washed her hands. The mango pickle would be ready for the palate after a week. If anybody got impatient and tasted it, they would baulk at the bitter-raw taste. Nothing in life can be hurried. Marriage or mango pickle. From the look and the aroma, she could tell that the pickle would be a great hit this time too. Her husband never ceased to wonder at this knack of hers. She would look at a dish, sniff it and declare it good or bad. "How on earth can you be so accurate?" he would gasp each time relishing her preparations. Rukmini believed it was her culinary expertise that had her husband eating out of her palms even after so many years of marriage. The pickling over and done with, kitchen cleared without a remnant of the activity, Andal went about getting the dinner organized. "Amma, should I make palakura mamsam for dinner?" she enquired. "You eat first, Andal. Look at you, you have thinned down so much," she said affectionately. Rukmini cared for her domestic help genuinely. But for them, her house would never have been a good home. She had been really fortunate that way. Nobody had left her ever, after her mother-in-law had passed away. When the old lady was alive, she had a tough time retaining anybody. Her language that turned foul along with her temper used to scare away the toughest of them. Even her son knew that. But every time she complained, he would shut her up. Her husband was a nice man but when it came to his mother he was a total wimp. A puppet in her hands. With a snap, she got him to do what she wanted.

Rukmini abhorred her mother-in-law but admired her for her hold on her family. But she hated her husband consistently when he behaved like a spineless character in his mother's presence. Thankfully, she had gone for good, God bless her soul, relieving her of pretences, once and for all. Now, she had him all to herself. That's what she had thought little realizing that her daughter would usurp his mother's position in their lives. Anyway, now even that was history. Menaka had got so wrapped up in her own drama that she had reduced her interactions with her father considerably. Especially after she split with Rishi.

Rukmini wondered at times why she felt nothing for her daughter except intolerance. Even as a kid, Menaka had been a tough cookie. Without her husband's help, God alone knew how she would have been able to deal with her first born. Coming to think of it, her daughter was very similar to her mother-in-law. Physically, she had inherited those earthy, sensual looks and temperamentally, the pig headed trait. And both had her husband dancing to their tunes. When it came to her, her husband was most rigid. She couldn't think of a time when he had indulged her the way he did his mother and daughter. Even now, with all the distractions gone, he rarely did, if ever, pay attention to her needs. But she had arrived at a truce with her placid existence that went on without a ripple. Her mother had prepared her well in advance to expect and accept such a situation in her life. She always told Rukmini not to depend on others for her fulfillment. "Don't look for a man's praise or you'll be left begging for it when it doesn't come." Luckily, her culinary skills had him addicted to her. Avakaya and gongura mamsam were his all season favorites.

Once the avakaya was declared ready by her, her husband would be the first one to sample it. He would pour generous amounts of pure ghee on steaming white rice and mix her bright red culinary creation for a dig in. The aroma of ghee and pickle combined with his undisguised relish was an appetizing sight for people who watched him at it. His daughter, when she was still with them, would be the only recipient of his delicious-as-heaven mixture. From the time she was two till she was 20, she would shamelessly devour every bit of the morsel that her father lovingly fed her. Rukmini couldn't still fathom how children change when they turn adults. Her daughter had turned her cynical towards the most sacred bond of the world. Luckily, her son hadn't let her lose hope. At least, not as yet. It would be nice to have another girl in this house. It would be nicer because the girl would be his son's wife. That would probably fill the emptiness that her daughter had left behind. She had to convince him to do it soon. Anytime now.

A few years back when she had taken ill during the season her trusted cook had tried her hand at avakaya making. After all, they had assisted amma for years and they felt they knew it all. Actually, they did a pretty good job of it but within a month little fungal growths were found floating one morning when they opened the lid. Turned out that the cook had used a slightly damp ladle to stir it around. That was the first and last time that Rukmini took chances with her speciality. She who was so finicky about everything that mattered to her had no inkling about her own daughter.

Rukmini often told herself that it didn't matter any more – her daughter's decision to elope. Her anger had reduced in its intensity but she could never forget her daughter's betrayal. It played in her head all the time like background music. She had felt a strange sense of victory when her marriage hadn't worked out but when she jumped into another marriage; she was concerned for her daughter. What was the matter with her? Menaka had always been reckless right from her childhood. Once, when she was around 6 or 7, Rukmini had chanced upon her daughter walking on the parapet. Menaka looked at her and smiled while continuing her walk on the edge. That sent a chill up her spine, she wanted to reach out, tell her to be careful, say she was concerned for her safety, yet she stood rooted to the ground unable to even extend her hand to her daughter. But Rukmini never told Menaka that she cared for her, was concerned about her safety. That continued to be her stance in the relationship. When you don't communicate what you feel to your close ones, chances are you alienate them for life. After all, the ability to express warmth through speech is unique to the human species. Rukmini's inability to express turned out to be her nemesis in her relationship with her daughter.

—⋗—

Prabhat was wondering how to put off his mother's drive to get him a bride. Something concrete had to be done. There was no way he could subject himself and a girl to the ridiculous ritual. But it seemed not just difficult but almost impossible. What to do? On an impulse he picked up the phone and dialed his sister's number. She answered almost immediately and enquired about him. He said, he was fine but needed her help in the matter of his marriage. She invited him over to her house for lunch and she said they could talk in peace because nobody would be home at that hour. Prabhat felt somewhat comforted. He had no clue what he would say to her but he also knew if there was a savior, it was her.

He landed at her house at half-past-one. The servant ushered him in and led him to the living room. The house was quiet. Almost eerie. It didn't feel like they were in a city. He could hear a crow cawing fervently right outside. After having been so busy, he wondered how his sister was leading such a quiet life. He had been to her apartment earlier when she was married to Rishi, which was far removed from this ambience. Rishi's colleagues were usually in their study; Menaka herself had friends almost all the time. Here the scene was like that of a holiday resort. Was she happy? As if on a cue, she walked in looking fresh but her eyes were red. As if she had cried. They hugged briefly and she broke down without a warning. As she continued to sob, tears came to his eyes. What was wrong? What had happened to his strong-at-times-ruthless sister? His heart melted. "I have ruined my life Prabha," she said as she disengaged herself from him. And then they sat next to each other. He moved away a little so he could look at her face. He waited for her to continue, "I shouldn't have left Rishi," she said and stopped abruptly. Prabhat didn't know how to respond, what to say. He just took her hands in his and said, "If you need my help, I am always there." She looked at him through her tear filled eyes and smiled weakly. "Thank you," she replied and regaining composure asked, "How come, you decided to grace me with your visit, li'l bro?"

"It's been a long time. Felt like seeing you," he said lying through his teeth. How on earth could he burden her with his problems when she was battling her own?

"Thank God," she said sounding almost normal, "I thought you had forgotten me completely."

The servant announced lunch and they moved to the dining room. A lavish spread greeted them. He was hungry and went about assuaging it with total concentration. They didn't talk much except how good the food was.

When they moved back to the living room he couldn't stop himself from asking, "What's the matter akka? Are you having problems with Dev?' Menaka turned quiet for sometime and then said, "I think I am having problems with myself. I don't know what I want."

Prabhat thought of something appropriate and finally came up with, "Well, we're all clueless, aren't we?"

"I guess," she said.

"You know sometimes I think life would be pretty boring if we all knew what we wanted and went about methodically getting it. It is the battle we have to go through to understand what we want that makes it interesting."

"You're probably right. Battling with society, people, conventions is all fine. There's a challenge in it that makes it worthwhile. But when there's one part of you battling with the rest of you, the conflict is killing."

"Why akka? Is Dev not okay with you?'

"I don't know anymore, Prabha, what's okay and what's not. I am so tired. Even when I was at the peak of my career working day and night, I never felt the kind of fatigue I'm experiencing now. You know, I left Rishi in a fit of anger. And anything done in anger is always followed by regret. I should have at least given it some time. But no, I rushed head long into this marriage. Now I feel lost. I don't know if I'll ever find myself again."

"I can imagine how that must be feeling."

Then she told him all about how Rishi's attitude bordered on insensitivity and how she met Dev when she was going through an all time low in her first marriage.

"You know akka, the biggest problem with us I think is that we never realize that nothing lasts. Every thing passes. Lows and highs. When we experience highs we want to hold on to them and when we experience lows we want to run away."

"You put it so well. Are you for real, Prabha? Can a man be so understanding and communicative? Seriously, tell me. I had almost written off men in that department. Unless of course, they're different. You know what I mean.'

Prabhat was dumbstruck. He turned quiet all of a sudden. His face turned pale. One look at him and she said, "Oh my God! Have I said something that's hurt you?'

"No Akka. You just spoke the truth."

"About what?'

"About me being different."

"What?!" she almost screamed but checked herself quickly, "Oh really? You're not kidding, are you?'

He shook his head. This time, she took his hands in hers and said, "That must be tough. Have you told anybody?'

He shook his head again.

Then they sat quietly. Menaka was trying her best to come up with the right things to say but couldn't. Prabhat was confused wondering if he had done the right thing by confiding in her. But a strange sense of relief flooded his being. He felt light. They shared a comfortable silence of confidence. This sharing of each other's conditions resulted in a bonding that they had never experienced in their lives so far. Life seemed liveable now. They sat like that hand in hand each unable to move away from the other. It was Menaka who stood up when she heard the gate opening to let Dev's car in. Quickly she whispered, "Don't tell him anything." He whispered back, "You think I'm crazy?" They smiled at each other conspiratorially. Dev walked in and was surprised to see the visitor and he said so. Within, he felt happy that finally Menaka was getting comfortable enough to invite her people home. So far, she had never had a visitor. He found it strange. When he had asked her that, she'd said, "I don't have friends." What about family, he wanted to ask but didn't. Now, he had the answer to the question he had never asked. Her brother had paid a visit, soon her parents would too. Finally, everything was falling in place perfectly. If only he knew!

After Prabhat left, Menaka tried to come to terms with his sexual orientation. It was difficult for her to comprehend how her handsome 6 ft brother could be different! He was unusually attractive, well mannered and cultured. He played cricket, polo and tennis. He swam and rode well, was a great dancer. In short, did all the things considered macho in the worldly sense of the term. But in retrospect she realized he had rare interests for an Indian man. He loved cooking. He spent hours in the kitchen on a Sunday trying out a new recipe or simply helping his mother. He also had great love for animals. He was seldom without a dog, usually several. His caring went beyond the normal playing and patting. He was very maternal towards them. He tended to them when they were sick; he showered generous doses of attention on them. She remembered how he sat through several nights if one of them wasn't well. Gardening was another passion. He reveled in growing flowering plants. And they responded beautifully to him. He also always was extra caring towards women in general. Which had made her think at that time that he possessed every asset that made a man, a complete one. She would often think how lucky the girl who gets him would be. Oh how sad! He would never experience normal life in that sense. But then who is she to define normalcy. Was she normal? Do normal women do stuff she did? Whatever makes one happy is ultimately what should be normal. For his sake, she sincerely hoped that he would be happy.

Her heart went out to her mother who would be shattered with his truth. It wasn't going to be easy for Prabhat, poor fellow! Had he come to her for help? As usual her self-obsessive nature hadn't even allowed that thought to come in when he was in front of her. She sat contemplating on life and its unpredictable ways, when Dev said, "Let's go out for dinner tonight." With Vaidehi, there was no question of dissent. But this woman was a different ball game altogether. She shot back, "For what?"

"Just like that. Do you need a reason to go out?'

"No, I'm not in a mood to."

"Well, you're never in mood to go out with me. What's new?'

"When you know it why do you ask?'

"Because I feel like eating out."

"So go."

"Alone?'

"Why, what happened to all those bimbettes you used to hang around with? Not to forget all those jobless, middle aged bachelor friends of yours"

"Yeah right! You're the only intelligent woman around."

"No, there are plenty. Only they are not around you."

"Why is everything an issue with you?"

"Because you make it that way."

"If this is the way you're going to respond, then I have nothing to say."

"You've nothing to say anyway. Except eating and drinking, you have no other interests."

Dev glared at her and walked into the bedroom. He would go out and show her. Show her what? He hadn't a clue. But go, he had to. What was she thinking? If only he had an answer for that question. She just wouldn't let him in. Sometimes he wondered why she had agreed to marry him. He had a niggling suspicion that she was seeing Rishi on the sly. If she was, then why had she left him? Maybe, this whole marriage thing was a mistake. Anyway, he needed a drink and he was going to get one. It was too boring to sit at home and have a drink all by himself. So he called Ashfaq who readily agreed to meet him at their favourite bar. While getting dressed, he realized that he was unable to get into half his clothes. That screwed up his mood further. He did, finally, find something to wear. He decided that he had to go shopping the next day. When he said bye to Menaka before leaving, she didn't even shift her eyes from the television and responded mechanically. He felt like strangling her for her indifference. He left hurriedly, got into the car and drove like a maniac. When he walked into the bar, Ashfaq was already there drink in hand. It was so good to see someone who was ready to be with him at any time he wanted. His mood lightened as he settled down and sipped his single malt. He loved his drink. Menaka made him feel like a worm every time he had a drink. She had told him once that she was not against alcohol per se, she herself enjoyed her occasional vodka, but she was against his drinking because he didn't know when to stop. Moreover, he was getting fatter by the day. "Hey Dev, trouble already or what?" Ashfaq enquired. "These women, I tell you, are beyond me!" he responded.

"Listen bugger," Ashfaq said, "I have told you this before and I am saying it again, it's very easy to keep them happy. All they ask for is a little attention. Okay, may be not a little, and may be a lot. But what the heck, man, why not? Don't you do that for your sons? I have seen you going crazy trying to please Karan who will sooner or later grow up and outgrow you."

Dev didn't respond. Ashfaq didn't press further. They got sloshed nicely and reached their respective homes past midnight. When he opened the door of the bedroom, Menaka stirred. He switched on the bed lamp to change. She picked up a pillow and covered her eyes with it making disgruntled noises at being disturbed. He derived sadistic pleasure and made some more noises opening and closing the cupboard. She got up and walked out banging the door shut. He quietly slipped under the blanket and dozed off. When he woke up in the morning and came out of the bedroom, the cook quietly brought his tea and newspapers. He walked into the balcony with the tea things, and didn't find her there. She wasn't in the loo either. Must be in the garden, he thought. That was one of her favourite places in the house. But there was no sign of her even after he finished his tea and polished off the newspapers. He came down to the ground floor and looked around. She wasn't there. He was about to walk out of the house to check in the garden when the servant realized he was looking for her and said, "Amma went out early in the morning." "Why didn't you tell me before?" he snapped at her and she grumbled something incoherent. At other such times he would have yelled at the top of his voice but now he didn't have the energy to. Quietly, he ate his breakfast wondering where she was. Unable to bear the suspense any longer he dialed her cell phone. It was switched off. That's it. All hell broke loose in his head and he decided enough was enough. He had to tell her in no uncertain terms that her behavior was unacceptable. She had to keep him informed. This wasn't a guesthouse or something for her to walk in and out as she pleased. He sat waiting for her without even bathing. She returned around noon and asked him, "How come? No work today?" He didn't reply. She walked past him without waiting for his reply and went up. Half-hour later, she came down dressed in jeans and a smart white kurti and said, "You're still here? I thought you had left for work. I am going out for lunch with my brother." This time, he looked at her and said, "Where were you all morning?"

"I was in the gym."

"For four hours?"

She looked at him angrily and walked out without responding. He followed her and repeated, "Were you in the gym for four hours?'

"Listen, my brother is waiting for me for lunch. We can talk later," she replied without looking him in the eye.

"I have been waiting for you too."

"Well, you didn't tell me."

"I didn't know I need to take an appointment from my wife to have lunch with her."

"How would I know you were planning to have lunch at home? I thought you'd be out as usual. When Prabhat asked me to have lunch at his hotel, I said yes."

And she was off.

Everything was an issue with this woman, he thought. With Vaidehi, life had been a smooth ride. But then, obviously, something had not been okay with their life. He wondered what. Ashfaq always told him that his rigidity was the root cause for his problematic relationships. May be he should change. But how? He was clueless.

Chapter XIII

Misery is like a strand of hair stuck on a bar of bath soap. Slippery and elusive. You think you've washed it off until you find it lurking on the other side.

Vaidehi's life after divorce had been exactly the way she had always wanted it to be. She was the mistress of all she surveyed and it gave her a sense of exhilaration she had never experienced during her life with Dev. Her mother had moved in with her post her father's death. It was a complete family, as far as Vaidehi was concerned. The only thing that jarred in her almost perfect life was Dev's weekend visit to fetch her sons to take them to his house. Much as she tried not to get disturbed, it did affect her. Today was one such Saturday when she was home and the boys were out with their father. Sometimes she felt cheated. All week when she was busy with work, she had to balance everything. And when she was free on weekends, eager to spend time with her sons, she didn't have them around. Life was nothing without them. Though she treasured her independence now, she knew she had to get a life. She was conscious of the fact that her life, though not really insipid, was missing something vital. She knew that her mind, though not crazy, was restless whenever she was on her own. Earlier her dreams, unfulfilled though, were what kept her alive. Of late, she had stopped dreaming for herself. And that was beginning to scare her slightly. To let go of dreams meant letting go of life. She knew she had to do something but she didn't know what. Was she missing the presence of a man in her life? But she panicked at the idea of going anywhere near one. Not again. One experience was enough to see what life was like with one. She wasn't going to give up this peace. Yet, sometimes she wondered how it would be if she had a man who was well, a man, in the true sense. A simple, straightforward man who valued a woman's presence in his life. Somebody who knew how to make a woman love the fact that she was a woman. Somebody who understood tenderness and passion. She also wondered if it was possible for her to love any man. She had felt none for the man whose children she had borne. She did feel nice and warm initially but Dev had successfully doused the passion, if there was any in her. He had tested the limits of her endurance. Limits of everything actually. She sighed and picked up a book from the rack. And she read

"It is unwise ... To hate all the roses because you got scratched by a thorn.
To give up on your dreams because one didn't come true.
To lose faith in prayers because one wasn't answered.
To give up on your efforts because one of them failed.
To condemn your friends because one betrayed you
To not believe in love because one was unfaithful or didn't love you back.
To not be happy because you didn't succeed on the first attempt.

Remember always...
Another chance
Another friend
A new love
Will come by...

She smiled and wondered if books had life and if they read her mind every single time she had a poser. She put it down to get ready for the evening.

After ages, she was going out to meet up with some old friends for lunch. She had a good mind to back out but she had nothing better to do. Moreover, she had to cultivate friends afresh. These two girls she was due to meet were her classmates from school. She had lost touch with them. Only recently they had reconnected on Facebook. Ritu, as she remembered had been her best friend until her parents had gotten transferred and moved to another city. The other girl Tina had been her closest rival when it came to the top rank in the class. A couple of times she had pipped her to the post, if she remembered right. God knows how this whole catching up business would turn out. Any which way, it was a good distraction and a better way to spend a Saturday afternoon than lazing around doing nothing except waiting for her sons to get back home. If not anything, it certainly was a better option than wondering if there was a better way to live life.

In an hour she was on her way to the Hyatt. When she entered the coffee shop, the manager greeted her and she asked him if somebody had left a message for her. That's what Ritu had told her on the phone because they were not too sure if they would recognize each other. She was led to the poolside table where she saw the two. They stood up smiling and hugged awkwardly. "I would have recognized you anyway," Vaidehi said settling down, "You still look the same. Actually more stunning. Wow, amazing!"

"Likewise," Tina said, "I think we should form a mutual admiration gang or some such thing."

It turned out to be a pleasant afternoon. They spent most of the time reliving their school days. After lunch, they ordered coffee and Ritu asked, "Listen Vaidehi, where were you hiding all these years? I mean Tina and I have continued to be in touch. In fact, we got closer after we left school. But you just disappeared, man."

"Did I? Never realized that. I guess I just got so involved with my higher studies. Moreover if you remember I wasn't really an extrovert."

"True. I remember you were the quietest girl in the class. By the way, what news of the others? Do you guys remember Lisa Varghese who had flunked in the 7th and became our junior?'

The other two did and said so.

"I met her recently at a hospital."

"Oh what happened to her?" Vaidehi asked.

"Nothing happened to her. I wasn't feeling well and she turned out to be the gynaec I was referred to."

"What are you saying?" Ritu exclaimed in disbelief.

"Yes, my dear, she's a doctor. Just imagine how we used to look down on her because she had flunked. I had even stopped talking to her because I thought I was this Miss Intelligent and talking to her was an infra dig. For a second I wondered if she would remember it. But she was very sweet. In fact, she was the one who recognized me instantly. I had this strange UTI issue and she was most caring. Obviously, she's really successful. I saw hordes of patients waiting for an appointment with her. Just imagine what crap we are brought up on."

"I tell you, our education system gives undue importance to this pass, fail nonsense." said Ritu.

The others agreed. The steward brought the bill and the tussle began.

"Ok, let's do one thing, let's go Dutch. Friendships last longer when people share, I believe.'

"We'll do that the next time," said Vaidehi grabbing the bill and passing it on to the steward with her credit card.

The other two gave in.

"By the way," Tina said as they picked up paan on their way out, "we haven't discussed anything of consequence. Ritu and I know about each other. Why don't we have coffee at the new coffee day outlet down the road?"

"Some other time," replied Vaidehi, "Time for my kids to get home. I need to get back."

"Why don't you tell their dad to get home earlier today?'

"Oh, it's their dad who would be dropping them home.'

"Didn't get that." Said Ritu.

"Well, their dad is not my husband any more. Get it?"

"Uh oh, I'm sorry," said Ritu.

"I am not," said Vaidehi and they laughed.

"We need to catch up soon, Vaidehi. I'm dying to share everything with you."

"Yeah sure. We'll stay in touch," promised Vaidehi as she drove out.

On the drive back, she really marvelled at her own candour. How easily she had disclosed the fact that she didn't live with her husband to them. She felt good. For the longest time, she felt some kind of reservation in talking about her marital status. But obviously, time had been the best strengthener. She was finally able to say it like it is with no qualms whatsoever. That made her feel really good. Almost like she had crossed a big hurdle. When her thoughts turned to the man she would have to see when she got back home, she was put off instantly. God! He'll maintain an expression like he's the best parent on earth and everybody else, mainly she, had no clue how to look after kids. And she was in no mood to endure that now. But she knew for sure that he would wait for her to return and leave only after making some caustic remarks. She had to get home before they arrived or else he would make her feel like garbage or at least make an attempt.

Surprisingly, Dev was in a good mood when he came in with the boys later in the evening. "Did you have a relaxed afternoon without these two breathing down your neck?" he enquired affably. She nodded and offered him tea. "I don't mind a drink," he said and quickly changed his statement when he noticed her hesitation, "Some other time. Actually, I have a party to attend."

Phew! There was no way she could be 'that' friendly with her ex. At least not yet. For some reason, she felt suffocated in his presence. Somebody had to tell him that he was too stuck up. She didn't know who would tell him. And if someone did she was certain he wouldn't believe that someone. Before the silence deepened he stood up to leave. When she said bye he smiled. Actually grinned broadly. From ear to ear.

"You look nice when you smile," she said.

"You never ever told me that when we were married."

"You probably never smiled like that."

"You think so? Strange, isn't it?" he said still smiling and suddenly without warning asked her, "Any boyfriend?"

She was too stunned to respond but managed to question back, "Have you found any one?"

"I did meet somebody interesting last night. But have not done anything about it yet."

"Good for you," she said aloud and wondered how anybody could fall for him. She pitied whoever the woman was. You never know, she felt, he was already smiling. There must be something in the woman, which brought out the lighter side of him. Suddenly, it occurred to her that if he remarried, her sons would have a step- mother. How strange that sounded! Little did Vaidehi know when she entertained these thoughts that it was she who would soon meet their future stepfather!

Menaka woke up with high temperature after a siesta. She was feeling kind of uneasy even as she was lunching with her brother. She thought sleep would settle it but it seemed to have made it worse. The moment she realized she was too weak to get up, she panicked. She was due to meet Rishi in an hour. She had to call him and tell him not to wait. She reached out for her cell phone and didn't find it on her bedside. When she stood up to look for it, her head spinned and she held on to the side table for support. Just then Dev entered the bedroom and rushed to her side. "God, you're burning with fever," he gasped while settling her back into bed. She closed her eyes too weak to respond. "Let me call the doctor. You lie down and don't move from here." He instructed and picked up the cordless. She didn't remember anything after that except that her entire body, head and throat ached and that occasionally she was woken up for a hot soup or medicines.

Rishi called her several times but her cell phone was off and when Dev answered the land line every single time, he hung up. Dev suspected who the blank caller could be. Rishi wondered what had happened to her. She had told him earlier how possessive that man was. Would he have locked her up? Could he? What kind of a man was he? That's when it occurred to him that he was indirectly responsible for her situation. He knew for a fact that she had loved him from the depths of her being. He had lost it somehow. He had taken her for granted. Her affection, her need for him and everything else that made a couple, couple-in-love. But how did she not, how could she not feel his love for her like she used to during the initial years. If only he could speak to her once. On an impulse he picked up the phone and dialled her landline. Dev answered again. Damn him! What should he do now? What could he do? There were two things he could do. Ask for her when he answers this time. Or he could land up at her house. He had never been to her house so far. He knew vaguely where she lived but it wasn't a big deal to find out. He could call the telephone exchange and get their address. He thought for a while and decided it was better to call on the phone than to take her unawares by landing up. He took a deep breath and rehearsed in his mind what he would say. The script came unstuck when he heard Dev's voice. "Hello," was all he could manage. When Dev said, "Yes?" he asked for her. Surprisingly, Dev said courteously, "She's down with virus. Who should I say called, please?" Rishi couldn't carry on any further and just disconnected abruptly. For a second, Dev looked at the phone before the caller's identity dawned on him. That's it. His mood completely went off. So his suspicion wasn't unfounded after all. His dear wife was meeting her ex-husband on the sly. His mind went completely blank before depression reared its tenacious head like an octopus and began spreading its tentacles. He looked at his wife who looked so baby-like in her sleep. He felt a surge of warmth that was immediately replaced by wrath. How could she do this to him? What had he not given her? She had every conceivable comfort and yet she was unable to snap ties with her past. He thought of his ex-wife who didn't bother to check if he was dead or alive. The only time she spoke to him was when he picked up or dropped the boys. That too, he thought, was more of a courtesy than anything else. So what was it that made this woman go back to him even after she had left him? Were they meeting every day? He went to her side of the bed and quietly took her mobile and walked out of the room. He switched it on and went through her call register. Every second incoming and outgoing call belonged to one number he didn't recognize. Obviously, she hadn't saved it on her phone. He contemplated if he should call the number to ensure it was Rishi's, but checked himself because he knew she would flare up. He had to think with a cool head now. Or else it could backfire and he would lose the battle even before it began. What was the right way to handle this situation? Rather a way that would swing the outcome in his favour. One thing was sure, it wasn't going to be easy. He had a good mind to confront her right now. He was in no mood to behave like a gentleman. He was hurt in his feelings, his pride.

While Dev seethed in anger, Menaka was in a world of her own with Rishi. He was touching her, stroking her, caressing her, fondling, teasing her, tantalizing her the way only he could. She was beseeching him to release her from the desire that made her ache from head to toe and everywhere in between. When he finally entered her, she convulsed with relief. The orgasm was real. She felt a surge of relief spread across her feverish body. She was sweating profusely as she opened her eyes. "Rishi," she called out weakly. Her voice was so soft - fortunately - that it was inaudible to the man who was in the adjoining bathroom. She sat up on her bed and found Dev opening the bathroom door. Her entire being rebelled at his sight and she felt a deep disappointment with herself. "How are you?" enquired Dev distantly still reeling, grappling with her betrayal. She nodded an okay for want of a better expression. "Would you like to drink something?" he continued politely. She said, "No, I am fine," this time. "That's good to hear," he said, "By the way some man called for you a little while ago but refused to divulge his name." "That must be Rishi," she blurted out. "How do you know?" he demanded. She didn't answer. He repeated his question. She closed her eyes. He walked out of the room. She drifted off to sleep and woke up after a while to a deep sense of unhappiness. She broke into uncontrollable sobs. Her body shook and her throat ached as tears kept rolling down her cheeks. Her pillow was completely soaked in her sorrow as her breakdown ebbed gradually. She felt totally drained, with not an iota of energy left in her body. She lay on her side staring out of the window. All she could see was wilderness of untamed shrubs. Not one leaf flickered. The world had come to a stand- still. She wanted to think something. Anything, but she couldn't. A vague sense of emptiness sat tightly in the middle of her stomach. Her mind was blank. Devoid of any feeling. God knows how long she lay there. Finally, her aching side woke her mind up. Or was it the mind that woke her up to her aching body? She sat up with difficulty and in walked Dev. She kept looking out the window. He walked across and stood in front of her. She was forced to look up at his face. She couldn't find any warmth in his expression. He looked grouchy and grumpy like his usual self. A surge of hatred spread across her insides. It must have showed on her face because Dev asked her, "You feel nothing for me?" and then as if he regretted having said that sat down next to her and put his arm around her, gently pushing her head on to his shoulder. She let it be. They sat in that position for a bit and then he said to her gently, "Listen baby, I think you should eat something now. You look pretty weak. Would you like to wash up or something?" She said, "Yes," and stood up with his support. Dev helped her into the bathroom and told her not to latch the door from within. He stood outside waiting for her to emerge but when he couldn't hear any sounds of the shower, he called her name softly. She didn't respond. He opened the door and found her lying on the floor. He picked her up in his arms, deposited her in the back seat of the car aided by the domestics and rushed her to the hospital. Her blood pressure had gone low, sugar level had dropped and she was put on a drip immediately.

Chapter XIV

Rishi called her home number and relaxed when somebody else answered the phone. His relief was replaced by anxiety when the voice over the phone - obviously of a servant's - told him that 'amma' was hospitalized the previous evening. Luckily, she told him the details of the hospital. He rushed to the hospital and located her room. When he walked in, it was a disturbing sight. Dev was helping her out of the bed and his back was towards Rishi. But when he looked at her face light up, he turned back too. Despite her weak state, she made a gesture to move towards Rishi and he rushed to her. She put her arms around him and began sobbing on his shoulder. Rishi stroked her head consoling her but she just wouldn't stop. Dev felt like an outsider in an instant. Rishi comforted her and guided her back to the bed. She held his hand like a child when he attempted to move away. He sat on the bed letting her hand rest in his, clutching gently. For a second, it felt like nothing had changed. She slumped back on her pillow totally exhausted by her physical condition and emotional outburst. When her breathing turned deep, he realized that she had gone to sleep. Only then did he turn to look at Dev who had turned ashen like he'd seen a ghost. An uncomfortable silence filled the room. Rishi stood up to leave and Dev followed him out. They didn't exchange a word until they were out in the corridor. Finally Rishi asked, "What's the matter with her?" Dev lied effortlessly, "Well, the doctors said it was a nervous break down. I suspect you are responsible for it."

"What makes you say that?" Rishi asked.

Dev improvised rapidly. Spinning yarns was his second nature. "Just before she fell ill, she told me that both of you had been meeting and she was beginning to get emotionally drained because she was feeling guilty. The day she fell ill she was supposed to meet you, wasn't she?" he asked.

Rishi hesitated to answer. Dev continued, "I know she was. When I told her that she was free to leave me if she wanted to get back to you, she said she had no such intentions but that she was seeing you because of her guilt. She said it was me she loved but she didn't want you to get depressed. I think you should assure her that you will do fine without her. You look perfectly alright to me."

"How I look is none of your business. Let me talk to her after she gets well."

"According to what she told me, you really made her unhappy. That's how she got involved with me in the first place. In fact, I used to tell her to try working it out for some more time but she said it was beyond redemption. Moreover, she said she was too tired working and fending for herself all the time she was with you. She's just about beginning to enjoy life Rishi, so I think you should leave her alone. Or the gentle soul that she is, she will never be able to tell you the truth. And look what it's doing to her. If you have any concern for her I think you should let her get on with her life. In any case, you have never had anything to offer her except misery and unhappiness. That's not my surmise, that's what she told me."

Rishi was too stunned to respond. Something was happening to him. He didn't know what but what he did know was that if this disgusting man continued to talk, he would strangle him. He quickened his steps and sped away without turning back to look at him. As he walked towards the parking lot, he was boiling with uncontrollable rage. His fingers trembled as he reversed the car. He banged into another car and when the watchman called out, he screamed his lungs off. He drove on autopilot and had no clue where he wanted to go. All he was conscious of was a need to run away from everything, everybody, every situation, and every relationship. Luckily for him, the traffic scene on the roads did not resemble his mental condition and he reached home safely. He remembered nothing of walking into his house.

He slumped into the sofa and before he was conscious of it he was sobbing uncontrollably. Only when it subsided, he tried to understand what hurt him so much. Was he feeling humiliated by another man or was he feeling let down by the woman he had loved so dearly? What Dev thought or felt about him was hardly of any consequence but how could she, no matter what the problems were in their relationship, confide in a stranger of sorts? Had she never felt any happiness with him ever in the years they had been together? How could that have been possible? For him, she had been the soul mate. It had never occurred to him that she wouldn't be with him. Ever! God knows he had loved her with all his being. There never was or could be anyone who would take her place. But obviously, she hadn't felt so intensely about him. But she had just clutched his hand so desperately in the hospital. He had felt her love. Of course, he had felt it. Was Dev making up the whole thing? He probably was. But then how could he have known such details if she hadn't told him. Where the hell had this man sneaked from into their near perfect life? Where had she met this ass? She had mentioned him fleetingly a couple of times like she mentioned countless others but he hadn't seemed important. Or was it his impression? Obviously, when you're in a marriage and you seek to have another relationship, there has to be something drastically lacking. Had it gone that bad? Why had he never seen it coming? Well, not that they didn't have issues. They did. But none that was insurmountable, right? Why had she thrown it all away? Agreed, he wasn't the best of husbands but he wasn't that terrible, was he? When he could love her the way she was, why couldn't she? Did he have nothing left in him? He sat thinking without switching on the lights even after it had turned dark. The door-bell startled him. Some silly bloke had rung the bell by mistake. He was looking for the person in 301 but he had landed at 201. He frowned but directed him to the right place. In a way, the man had interrupted his agonizing thoughts. He decided the best thing to do now was to visit the British Library. Books are the only diversion that helped him get a break from his mind's relentless activity.

He had a quick shower and was out in ten minutes. He stopped his car at a distance behind a reversing car hoping to park in its place. He briefly saw a pretty face before she brushed against the side of his car in some strange quirk of wheels. Before he could respond, she halted the car and walked to him and said, "I am really sorry. I just hate driving and it shows every time I am forced to." He laughed saying, "Thank God, I thought I must have done something to deserve this." She laughed too and said, "Thanks for being so cool." He said, "No sweat, happens to the best of us." When he parked the car and got out after locking it he found her at the same place struggling with the door. He stood watching as she removed a pin from her hair and tried fiddling with the door. He realized that she had locked herself out of her car. He walked up to her and said, "Since we drive the same model, I suppose my key could help. If you could just let me, I can try." She moved aside with knotted brows. "Relax," he said to her, "No big deal. Worst case scenario, we'll get a mechanic."

"I know but I feel terrible that I may jam the traffic."

"That's what you call a jam session."

She smiled. He did something and the door opened smoothly.

"What did you do?" she asked astonished.

"Trade secret. I make a living as a part time car thief." He looked at her bewildered expression and continued, "Don't look so shocked. I am just kidding. Like I said, I drive the same model. We just got lucky."

As he opened the door for her, he noticed the book that was on the passenger seat. When she said, "I don't know how to thank you," he replied, "I can think of one way. You could pass on the book to me before you return it. I have been looking for it for ages."

"Actually, you can take it now. I can wait."

"That's wonderful. How do I return it to you?'

She took out the visiting card holder from her bag and gave him her card. "You can call me when you're done." He cast a cursory glance and put it in his shirt pocket. He walked towards the library as she drove out. They were oblivious of the smiles on their faces or each other's.

Prabhat learnt about his sister's illness when he called her residence after trying her mobile phone which was turned off. Concerned, he landed at the hospital. As he was about to step into the room, the scene that greeted him assaulted his senses. Menaka was lying on the bed, visibly week and ill. Dev was talking to her in a raised voice and questioning her about something. Prabhat could sense his sister's humiliation even as she lay there in no position to respond.

He cleared his throat and Dev turned back. On seeing Prabhat, he changed his expression and smiled. "Come, come. I am glad you are here. Your sister has been giving me a hard time refusing to eat. Now that you are here, I am relieved. Actually, you two talk. I'll pick up some fruits and come back in a jiffy." He said and walked out.

Prabhat sat next to his sister and held her hand. She smiled weakly and closed her eyes. He knew this was not the right time to ask her any questions but he surely would once she got well. If she had issues, whatever they may be, he would stand by her. From what he saw, he had no respect left for Dev. Obviously, it wasn't about her refusal to eat. And whatever else it may have been, nothing warranted talking down to somebody who was so unwell. That too, to one's life partner. Somebody had to tell Dev that Menaka wasn't alone. And that somebody had to be him. What kind of a man would talk to his ailing wife in a raised voice? The more he thought, the more agitated Prabhat got.

Dev decided to pick up fruits from home. As he honked incessantly at the gate, the servants sprang into action dropping whatever they were engaged in at that moment and one of them, Yadagiri, the mali ran to open the gate for the master. Dev drove in, rolled the car window down and hurled abuses at Yadagiri, cast aspersions on his mother's character, wondered about his wife's morality, all because the gate wasn't opened at the sight of his car. Yadagiri stood with his head down swallowing his self respect and dignity.

The rest of them looked on helplessly until Dev yelled at them too and they disappeared, not wanting to incur his uncontrollable wrath and verbal onslaught. Once earlier when Yadagiri had dared to explain his action, Dev had gotten out of the car and beaten him mercilessly. After that incident, Yadagiri had learnt his lesson. The only reason he stayed in this job was because he lived with his wife, Rani and three daughters in the servants' quarters. At least his family had the security of food and shelter here. Back in his village, his parents struggled to make ends meet. Water was scarce and the land was parched. No farm had any significant yield for years. Thanks to this job, he was able to send his parents some money every month. At least, they didn't have to go hungry. His wife, Rani, washed clothes and vessels and together they somehow consoled each other. Once when Dev's handkerchief hadn't been washed to his satisfaction, he summoned her to wash it again. It was dinner time and she had just about begun feeding her two year old daughter who had been suffering from fever. But the moment she heard Dev's voice, she washed her hands and ran to do his bidding. Yadagiri had gone out to pick up medicines. By the time the parents returned from their chores, the girl had fainted from weakness. That day, Rani had sobbed uncontrollably cursing her fate. For the umpteenth time, Yadagiri died of guilt for subjecting his family to such helplessness.

Later, when Menaka had learnt about the incident, she had threatened Dev that she would walk out if he ever, ever again behaved so cruelly. Dev couldn't figure out why Menaka always supported the servants. These incompetent louts, fit for nothing people, two bit domestics had more respect in her heart than him. Coming to think of it, his ex-wife too had picked up fights with him for the sake of their servants. Something was terribly wrong with women, he decided. How could they fight with him for those low life servants? He wondered seriously.

Chapter XV

When Dev returned, Menaka asked for her cell phone. He told her it was a bad idea to exert herself. She closed her eyes out of sheer weakness though she wanted to speak to Rishi. Dev peeled some oranges and fed her, speaking gently as if she were a baby. It felt nice, actually, to be looked after. Disease brings out the child in us. Wanting to be held, cooed to, taken care of…And if we don't find caring at such times, we feel vulnerable like a kid who has lost track of his parent.

In the days that followed, Dev took care of her every need before she asked. In a strange way, she felt gentler about him too. More often than not, it's these small gestures that result in attachment between two people. Receiving and giving are incomplete in isolation.

When she got back home, Yadagiri, Rani, their children, the dogs rushed to greet her. Rani had brought out the silver plate with red vermilion mixed in water to ward off the evil eye. She circled it around Menaka thrice and discarded the water in the Tulsi plant. The Tulsi plant is a regular fixture in every Hindu household. The scientific reason being that by virtue of inhaling and exhaling oxygen, Tulsi purifies the environment much more than other plants. "That's quite a reception committee," Menaka smiled weakly feeling good about being welcomed so warmly. Dev realized how much every person in his household had taken to Menaka. He actually felt so left out when the whole tamasha was going on. He told Rani, "Enough of this naatak now. Amma needs to rest for a couple more days." Everybody backed off and retreated to their respective chores.

Menaka felt good being back in her bed. Familiarity is so comforting, so secure. With Dev's constant monitoring of her diet and rest, she bounced back to her old self. Why wasn't Rishi calling, though? She drifted off into the land of the subconscious and was woken up suddenly. She forced her eyes open and saw a hairy arm tapping her on the back of her palm. When she looked up it was her tormentor still a hazy form but below the neck from shoulders downward till the torso, the bare body was that of Rishi. Bewildered she looked down. The lower half of the body with long legs had trousers on with a belt and shoes on the feet that belonged to Dev. Before she could register what was going on both the hands held her by the armpits and started pulling her up in the air. But her lower half wouldn't move. When she looked down at her own body, she saw that it was being held down by Dev's long legs that were somehow pinning hers down hard. While the arms pulled her up, the legs couldn't move. With one strong pull, Rishi's arms yanked her upper half detaching it from the lower half. Her body was in two pieces now. Upper half held in the air by Rishi's arms under her arm pits and lower half held in position by Dev's long legs. Even as she stared in shock, the body of the hazy form got divided into two too. Rishi's upper half in the air detached from Dev's legs. She excruciating pain and cried out loudly. That's when she heard Dev's voice repeating her name. She opened her eyes and realized her nightmares were now losing track of time and appearing during the day too. She clung to Dev helplessly. "Please help me. I can't take this anymore." He hugged her tight and she felt comforted immediately.

Chapter XVI

When you close doors on new experiences, life is like a black & white motion picture. You get the story but miss out on the colours...

Rishi went through complete metamorphosis after Dev's revelations in the hospital. He decided there was no point in hanging on to the vestiges of a dead relationship. He was finally ready to move on. On the way back from his office he stopped at his regular liquor store and picked up cans of Budweiser. His idea of alcohol was beer. Period. He had never really taken to whisky, vodka or rum. It was Saturday evening and he intended chilling out at home with Budweiser and Vaidehi for company. She had called earlier to check if he had finished reading the book as it was overdue to be returned to the library. He had asked her if she wanted to drop in for a drink later in the evening. She had agreed without any drama. He had had enough of one woman who said something, meant something and did something else altogether. Such a relief to meet someone who was simple and straight. He had decided to put some semblance of order back into his life after Menaka had thrown it into complete disarray. In a way, it was good she was never interested in having children. Strangely, even though they never really practiced safe sex, she had never become pregnant. Once when she had missed her period, she had panicked. She was almost in tears and kept blabbering, `I hope not, I hope not' and that's when he realized that there was something amiss. It was already 5 years since they had been married and she was close to 26 while he was 32. He was quite settled in his job and so was she. More importantly, he adored children.

He had asked her, "Don't you want to have kids ever?" She had done her usual thing of being wishy washy. With her, there were no clear answers for any questions. How she had the clarity to walk into his house to get married, only she knew. "Are we ever going to have children?" he persisted and she had said, "Oh come on, don't go on and on about it now. Please. You're getting on my nerves."

"Getting on your nerves is my full time occupation, you see," he had retorted, exasperated.

He had reached his apartment block. As he parked in his lot, Bahadur came running to see if he needed any assistance. This guy, Bahadur, was a Nepali working as the security guard since the time Rishi and Menaka had occupied this flat. Rishi and Menaka were always nice to people indulging in friendly banter with their domestics and whoever else worked for them. They were also generous tippers. It was best of both the worlds. Money and respect. Nobody who worked for them wanted to ever leave them. Bahadur was disturbed for days after he had realized that Menaka wasn't travelling but had left for ever. He felt very protective towards Rishi and would take extra care to see to it that his Saab was comfortable. "Kya Bahadur, sab theek," Rishi enquired as he got out of the car. Bahadur said, "Haan saab," and took the carry bag from his hand. Rishi walked into the elevator with Bahadur following him. It was a normal routine for them every evening on Rishi's return no matter what the time happened to be. In fact, a few other owners would scream at Bahadur for doing Rishi's work on higher priority but he couldn't care less. He felt genuine affection for this man. Casually, he enquired, "Guests Saab, tonight?" Rishi said in a conspiratorial tone, "Yes, one lady guest," and winked at him. Bahadur chuckled. Rishi was probably the only man he had seen who was always light hearted. He was also probably the only man who spoke to him like a friend. Once Rishi unlocked the main door, Bahadur walked in and arranged the beer cans in the fridge. "Saab, call me if you need any help," Bahadur told Rishi who was serving himself a glass of water, and left. Rishi took his wallet out from his back pocket and gave him a 100. Bahadur grinned, saluted and exited.

Rishi went into the kitchen, took the bowls and plates out from the top compartment of the built in cupboard, got the spoons and forks out and arranged them on the dining table adjoining the kitchen. It wasn't a huge flat by Hyderabad standards. Two thousand sft but he felt it was more than enough for two people. Menaka had also loved this place. In fact, every inch of the flat had her signature. She had a flair for getting these things right. He had learnt a lot by observing her and now it was coming in handy. He surveyed everything once and went in for a shower. The bathroom wasn't huge either but it had a neat glass shower compartment on the right, wash basin in front of a wall length mirror and pot on the left corner. Several times, when they had to go out, they would shower together ostensibly to save time. Once under the shower, he would somehow end up inside her. It had turned habitual almost.

He had a quick shower and got out with the towel around his waist. Just as he got into his shorts and T shirt, the bell rang. He looked at the clock and realized that it had stopped. "Must get it repaired," he told himself the zillionth time. The bell rang again and he rushed to open it. At the other side of the door stood their old maid servant who had vanished just before Menaka had left. He couldn't remember her name but smiled. She told him that she wanted to come back to work if he was okay with it. By then her name sprang to his mind – Durga. He asked her to come in and while he was listening to her chatter, Vaidehi walked in. Durga looked at her and enquired, "Oh Saab, I totally forgot, where is amma?" In no mood to explain, he told her that she was travelling. She cast another surreptitious glance at Vaidehi and left after telling him that she will start work from the next morning.

He turned to Vaidehi and said, "I am so sorry for that distraction. Please make yourself comfortable. I will just get the drinks out."

"Cool," she said, "I could see you were busy with a new recruitment."

"Nah, not new," Rishi replied standing in front of the open fridge contemplating, "Old one. Just resurfaced after disappearing without any explanation or information. I seem to have a knack of attracting people who come and go and then come back as and when they please."

Vaidehi was amused that he had so much philosophy for a truant domestic help. She saw him still standing in front of the fridge scratching his chin and asked, "Any help?"

He said, "No, just wondering if I should make a salad for you."

She said, "Don't bother. Let's go out for dinner."

He said "okay," and brought the cans, plates and bowls of chudwa (Savory snack) and cashewnuts in a tray.

"You're too cool, I say," said Vaidehi, "Must say you're quite self sufficient."

"Advantages of being married for a long time or should I say divorced?"

An uneasy silence hung in the air. Vaidehi took in the ambience. It was a sweet place. Everything well organized and well kept for a man who was living alone.

Rishi passed on a can of beer to her and they spoke about inane stuff. Light and easy conversation followed as did more cans of Budweiser. As the spirit went down, their spirit went up. They reveled in an easy comfort inexplicably considering they had barely known each other before. For a change, Rishi's mind didn't go to Menaka and Vaidehi didn't rue about lonely weekends. Hours passed and they realized that it was way past midnight and it occurred to them that the restaurants would be shut. Worst thing about Hyderabad was that everything shut by 11.30. Cops were pretty strict barging into eateries to enforce the law. Only five star coffee shops were open. But Rishi knew a low profile place in Basheerbagh that served midnight biryani. She was game to try it out. With copious amounts of beer in his blood stream, Rishi didn't want to risk getting a breath analyzer shoved down his mouth, so he called Jahangir, the driver who lived right behind the apartment block. Soon they got into the backseat of Rishi's car while trusted Jahangir sat behind the wheel. It was quite a long drive. For the first few minutes, they sat looking out their windows lost in their own heads. Rishi cleared his throat and Vaidehi looked at him. Their eyes met and she felt electricity pass through her veins. He looked deeply into her eyes and asked, "Did you feel that?" She just sat transfixed. When he bent forward and placed his right hand on her left, his touch was feverish and she felt the heat spread through her being. When he raised it to his lips, she thought she was going to burst into a million pieces. Never before had she experienced such a rush of blood. The rest of the evening went by in a haze. They could feel the sexual tension build up while Rishi polished off his biryani and Vaidehi helped herself to a few spoons from his portion. They barely spoke on the way back. When they reached his place, she got off and went straight to her car which she had parked outside the gate of his apartment building. "Why don't you come up for coffee?" he asked her and she said, "I am not ready for it yet." He didn't pursue, just stood there with his arms crossed at his chest and watched as she unlocked the door and got into her car. As she drove back, her mind was blank, in a daze. When she walked into her home everything was quiet, but the hectic activity in her heart told her that an important phase, a very significant experience, was opening its portals for her. The man she had just met had the potential of letting her throw caution to the winds. She was no longer a woman who guarded her emotions inside an iron heart. Something had changed. She could feel it.

Rishi got into the elevator and turned the key into the door lock of his house whistling a happy tune. He couldn't remember when he had felt this light hearted. Not even during his happily married phase. Menaka didn't have the knack of making a man feel comfortable. She drove him crazy, got him addicted to her body but never ever put him at ease. On the contrary, he was always on tenterhooks around her, walking on egg shells, feeling inadequate, not being able to measure up, always trying hard to live up to her expectations.

From that night to this afternoon when they were in bed together, feeling each other's comforting presence, a few months had passed. They shared an easy equation. She wasn't a tigress in bed, she was subdued, almost like a recipient of his affection and passion. They didn't challenge each other in any way; they were just happy to be in their spaces and their space together. He had met her sons; she had brought them over to his house the first time. They had taken their time but had warmed up to him. They would go out to dinners and movies as a family and this is precisely what they were missing. He had never experienced biological fatherhood but this was the closest he had come to as far as caring as a parent was concerned. For her, Rishi was the ideal dad. Unlike Dev's controlling, oppressive ways, Rishi was gentle and effortless with her sons. They had already started missing him, enquiring when they would be seeing him again. Dev had informed her that his wife was unwell and he had to be by her side, which had given them more time to be together over weekends. Life had become far more interesting and energizing for all of them. Rishi and Vaidehi knew that the time had come to move to the next level but neither of them took the first step. But on that day, when they were soaking in the beautiful sense of togetherness, with Vaidehi in his arms with her face on his chest, Rishi spoke up. "So what next Vai," he asked her, "and don't say why Vai," he said with his characteristic impulsive cover up of a serious matter with a joke. That is what she loved about him. His ability to laugh at everything. For a serious person like her, he was the perfect foil.

"I will not ask why Rishi but how is my question?" she said earnestly. "Maybe we should get married. What do you think?" he asked. This was the best part about him. He always sought her opinion. He always gave more importance to what she felt. They were equals, at times she even felt superior. "I am not sure how the boys will take it, Rishi. They have grown to love you, for sure but I don't know how they'll take to it. And how their father would react." "Well, I know for a fact that I can never be their father. I have never and never will try to replace him. That's the reason I asked them to address me by my name. Not even uncle. And moreover you said he has remarried, right? You have every right to do so too." Vaidehi never spoke about her husband. She never mentioned his name. The boys would occasionally talk about Papa but that was it. Rishi wasn't so bothered either. Her past was hers. If she felt like sharing something she obviously would. He had never been the inquisitive kind. That was also one of the reasons she was so much at ease with him. "It's not about my right to move on Rishi," she looked into his eyes as he waited for her to complete her sentence when the door bell rang. He wondered who it could be at that hour in the afternoon. He wasn't expecting anyone. He tried ignoring it hoping that whoever it was would go away. But she got out of bed and started getting dressed. He said, "Come back," in a bid to continue the conversation but the bell rang again, this time repeatedly. She said, "Please go and check. I will wait here," she said and sat back on the bed picking up a magazine that was lying on the bedside table. He put on his jeans and walked out bare chested with the intention of sending the visitor away. It was probably the milkman or the watchman. He unlocked the door and opened it slightly to tell the visitor to come later. But when he saw who it was all his reflexes shut down and he just stood there. Menaka pushed the door ajar walking in saying, "What took you so long to open the door? I have been ringing the bell forever. And why didn't you call even once to check how I was? You visited me just once in the hospital. After seeing my condition also, you didn't even bother? Somehow, I managed to get out. Dev wouldn't let me step out alone." Rishi had shut the door and was leaning on it listening to her tirade. His brain had shut down the instant he had seen her. She was heading to the bedroom when he suddenly came to his senses and rushed to stop her. But she had already walked in. He hadn't even shut the bedroom door in his hurry to send the visitor away. Menaka looked at the woman sitting on her bed reading a magazine. Vaidehi looked up and saw her. It took a little while for both the women to recognize each other as they had met just once though Menaka had seen Vaidehi's pictures. For a while nobody spoke. Rishi cleared his throat and said, "Vaidehi, this is Menaka, my ex-wife. Minnie, this is Vaidehi, my future wife though she hasn't said yes yet." Menaka replied, "Are you out of your mind Rishi? I know Vaidehi. She is Dev's ex-wife. How on earth did you both meet? And when did this happen. Till the time I was hospitalized you were with me. In just three months everything has changed. You actually decided to marry another woman in such a short time?" Menaka went hysterical, ballistic as she hyperventilated. Rishi tried calming her down by putting his hands on her shoulders and she pushed them away with force. She walked out in a huff, out of the apartment, out of his life. That's when Vaidehi found her voice and said feebly, "She didn't seem well at all Rishi. Maybe you should see if she's okay." Rishi ran down the steps without waiting for the elevator and saw Menaka being driven away in a chauffeur driven car. He just stood there akimbo panting. Looking at him, the watchman came running and enquired, "What happened saab? Memsaab just went away!" Rishi just nodded his head from side to side and got into the elevator which was left ajar by Menaka. He pulled the old fashioned elevator's grill doors and when it started moving up, everything came back to him in flash. "Oh hell! Vaidehi was Dev's ex-wife? Holy mother! How did this happen?" The door to his apartment was still open and Vaidehi was sitting on the sofa in the living room staring into space. When he obstructed her vision, she looked up and said, "What is this Rishi? What have we done? How did this happen? And what did she mean by you were with her till three months ago? Weren't you divorced long back and she remarried Dev?" Rishi just sat next to her and put his arm around her shoulder. She leaned against him. After a brief pregnant pause, Rishi narrated everything to her and ended it with, "If you hadn't come into my life and if we hadn't fallen in love, three lives would have been caught in a deathly warp. I had fallen out of love with her long ago but somehow she had a hold on me and whenever she came to me, I let her do whatever she wanted. In fact, I was so miserable and lonely that eventually, I would have killed myself." She raised her fingers to his lips and said, "I know what you mean. I am glad we found each other." "Does that mean you said yes to marriage? Our marriage?" he asked. She nodded in affirmation and said, "But we have Dev to deal with. He is a very complicated man. He will try his best to take the boys away. That's what I wanted to tell you before she walked in." "Yeah, I know. Heard all about him from Menaka," he said pensively. "What? They are not happy together? Obviously not! That's why she was still seeing you. God, what a mess!" she exclaimed. He said seriously for a change, "Mess or hell, we shall face it together." She smiled and nodded. "Time to pick up the boys from school. Come let's go," he said looking at the watch on his left wrist and pulling her up to her feet with his right hand. She stood up clutching his hand tight.

Chapter XVII

The driver Yaqub was clueless about what he should be doing. Menaka was sobbing uncontrollably in the backseat. A couple of times he asked her where to go but she hadn't heard his question. She continued crying. He halted the car to a side and offered her the bottle of water saying, "Madam, Please drink water. You haven't been well for three months. It's not good for you to cry so much." Menaka raised her head, saw him and composed herself a bit. She drank water, opened the car door and splashed some on her face. When she sat back in her seat, he stood out patiently, waiting for her to call him. After regaining composure, she called out to him. He sat back in his seat, waiting for her instructions. She asked him to head to Birla Mandir. Yaqub was surprised. Madam had never been one to visit temples or holy shrines. That too to a touristy destination like Birla Mandir, a Hindu temple, built in 1976 on a 280 feet high hillock called *Naubath Pahad* on a 13 acres plot. The construction had taken 10 years to complete and was a huge attraction for devouts and ex pats. The residing deity Lord Venkateshwara was known for granting wealth. Yaqub wondered why she chose to go there when they already possessed enough wealth. From his perception, she needed health and peace right now. But God knows what goes on in their lives and minds. Out of the blue he said to her, "Madam, I know a dargah where sufis gather on Thursdays and sing. The place and the music are known for their healing powers. Would you like to go there now?" Menaka mulled over it and said okay. As luck would have, it was Thursday. She just had to go somewhere right now where she wouldn't be disturbed with the need for inane conversations. She needed to process what she had seen. Her heart was in deep turmoil and her mind was numb. All she could feel was shock and hurt.

Yaqub informed her it would take an hour and a half to get there and began his drive to the outskirts of Hyderabad through the old city. She looked outside the window when her cell phone began ringing. It was Dev. She had to answer the phone though she was in no mood to talk to him. "Hi Dev," she tried to sound as normal as she could. Obviously, he was concerned as today was the first day she had ventured after three long months of being in hospital and home. She told him she was going to the Sufi dargah which was the truth. Luckily, he didn't ask her anymore questions except when she would be back and she had said around 9 ish.

En route to the dargah, she saw the setting sun. By the time they reached, moonlight had begun to spread its silvery hues all around. The dargah was located in a quiet area away from the noise and din of the city. It was a full moon night in a magical zone of its own. As they entered the portals they saw quite a few people seated on white mattresses on the floor. On a corner was a group of musicians, all of them had deep kohl lined eyes. Two of them on the dholak had long flowy silky dark hair upto their shoulders, one of them who occupied centre stage - obviously the main singer - was a striking looking young man barely in his thirties with a piercing gaze she saw for a fleeting moment before he went into a trance. Menaka settled down with Yaqub who had accompanied her to be there if she needed any help. She looked so frail that he felt protective and responsible for her well being. The group tuned their instruments and the rendition was begun by the young singer. In the next couple of hours, Menaka had lost track of the entire world, her life and all people in it. She was transported to another realm with the divine music filling the air and the fragrance of dhoop (aromatic gum of a tree) wafting in it. When she came to, which was after the music had stopped, she looked at her cell phone which was on silent mode and heaved a sigh of disappointment that there were no phone calls. She had somewhere expected Rishi to call at least to explain if not pacify. Everybody started walking out and she followed them with Yaqub by her side. Music had an amazing therapeutic effect, she realized for the first time in her life and thanked Yaqub for the experience. He said he was glad that he could be of some help.

The time was 7 PM when they got into the car for the drive back. Strangely, there were no calls from Dev either. She was in no mood to talk to anybody in any case. Just as well. On the drive back, when the finality of what she had witnessed in Rishi's apartment hit her, she felt hugely remorseful at the way she had treated Dev. She decided that from now on she would respect him for what he is and accept the love he had for her. That he loved her to death was obvious. From day one, he had been clear about his intentions towards her. It was she who had been indecisive, vacillating and irresponsible towards him and their relationship. Now that Rishi had woken her up to reality, she would take charge of her life. What Menaka didn't know was that life had decided its own course. Life was in no mood to give her any chance to put her thoughts into action. It was the proverbial calm before the storm. Little did she know that the man she was planning to make amends with would be in no position to give her that chance. Once lost, gone forever!

In the days that followed Dev's death all that Menaka could do was cry. Tears of regret, remorse, pain, anguish washed her being constantly. Vaidehi had come with her kids, Dev's sons, to the funeral. The elder one, Menaka's heart went to the young boy, had lit the pyre. Vaidehi had been more than nice to her, almost like the sister she never had, making sure she ate and rested without any disturbance. Menaka barely came out of her room while Vaidehi handled all their relatives and friends who were home on the condolence visit. She took charge of the kitchen, feeding people during ceremonies for 13 days that followed. She took off from work and stayed there to be with her regardless of what people thought or spoke. Menaka couldn't help wondering how Dev could have left such a wonderful woman and realized that it was Vaidehi who had left him.

After a month, one day when Menaka was sitting on the bench in her garden watching the boys playing with the dog, Vaidehi approached her and asked her if she could sit next to her. Menaka said, "What kind of a question is that? Please do. But for you, I wouldn't have been able to get through this. I have no words to thank you." Vaidehi sat next to her saying, "Come on, he was the father of my kids. This was the least I could do. Maybe it was my farewell gesture to him. I did it for my own sake." In the little time they had spent, Menaka had understood that Vaidehi was a woman of few words but whenever she spoke, her words had an air of tranquility. Menaka resumed the conversation saying, "You know, I was so confused and angry the day I had seen you at Rishi's and when he said that he was in love with you but now I can see why. I also know that he's going to be very happy with you. By the way, where is he?" Vaidehi replied, "He's too scared to face you. You know him better than I do, I am sure. I don't have to tell you he can't face confrontations or unpleasantness. He's an escapist of sorts. But he wanted me to let you know that he does want to see you if it's okay with you." Menaka was speechless. A woman who knew him for a few months was justifying the behaviour of a man who was married to her for a decade. To add to that, the man she thought she was closest to was conveying his message through her! Wow! Does that have anything to do with them or was it her own lack of understanding of people? It felt weird but she somehow managed to ask her to let Rishi know that he was most welcome to visit her. She didn't know if she could meet him with a straight face but she was ready to face him now. She was anything but an escapist. She was impulsive, foolish, acted first and thought later, but never tried to escape a situation.

Rishi came the next day. They looked at each other uncomfortably. Menaka could sense the ease he shared with Vaidehi and the boys. How strange that Dev's sons' step parents were a married couple before they met their parents! And then, the inevitable happened. The incident that killed her pride, ego, self respect and everything in that zone. Rishi walked away with Vaidehi and Dev's kids; he had actually come to pick them up. Vaidehi was obviously being polite when she said he had wanted to see her. Obviously they couldn't have stayed here forever, but still. After they left looking like one happy family, Menaka sat there feeling like an alien in her skin, like a stranger in her own home. The man who had brought her to this house was no more. And the man who had driven her to this home had just walked away with his beloved and her husband's kids as if they were his own. Life! In that twilight, on that day, she decided that she had to understand what she was made of. Who was this woman sitting there, watching her ex-husband walking out of her home with her dead husband's ex-wife?

So that's how Menaka landed in Pondicherry still being plagued by her tormentor and her past. She knew that these long walks on the beach, this running away from her own home, were not permanent solutions. She knew there had to be something to fall back on. Like a relationship, family, kids, but she had none of these. Her only family was the one she was born into. But her parents had disowned her. Her brother hadn't called her even once after the funeral. Strange because she had thought they had rediscovered each other and that their bond had strengthened. What was weirder was that her most trusted domestic help – Yadagiri and his wife had left for their village after Dev's death citing some unavoidable family emergency. Why had everybody decided to desert her when she needed them the most? Was there anybody who would help her find peace and happiness? "Yes, me," she heard a voice right behind her. When she turned back she saw the hazy form repeating the words, "Only I can make you happy, Menaka. Come embrace me. Own me. Don't treat me like your enemy. Unless you make me your best friend, you won't be able to survive." Menaka ran as fast as she could, away from the hazy form. She was alarmed that she saw her tormentor with her eyes wide open this time. She wasn't asleep. The line between dreams and reality had disappeared. She couldn't tell one from the other?

The next morning she checked out of her room. She had enquired through the hotel's information desk if she could find a place where she could learn meditation. They had guided her to a workshop that was being conducted by a new age guru. But the condition of the person she spoke to over the phone to register was that it was a residential workshop and you had to stay there for 15 days. The place was called Auroville. She had booked her accommodation in a self contained studio in the centre which was within a kilometer away from Auroville.

She hired a cab and reached there in about an hour. She was guided to the vistors centre building, where she walked around reading the literature for visitors there.

"Auroville wants to be a universal town where men and women of all countries are able to live in peace and progressive harmony above all creeds, all politics and all nationalities. The purpose of Auroville is to realise human unity."

Auroville Charter

1. Auroville belongs to nobody in particular. Auroville belongs to humanity as a whole. But to live in Auroville, one must be a willing servitor of the Divine Consciousness.
2. Auroville will be the place of an unending education, of constant progress, and a youth that never ages.
3. Auroville wants to be the bridge between the past and the future. Taking advantage of all discoveries from without and from within, Auroville will boldly spring towards future realisations.
4. Auroville will be a site of material and spiritual researches for a living embodiment of an actual Human Unity.

Fascinating, she thought! How could she not have known of the existence of such a heaven on earth. Where you come from is of no importance. As she read more from the brochures, she realized she had finally found her sanctuary.

What is Auroville?

Auroville is a universal township in the making for a population of up to 50,000 people from around the world.

How did Auroville begin?

The concept of Auroville - an ideal township devoted to an experiment in human unity - came to the Mother as early as the 1930s. In the mid 1960s the Sri Aurobindo Society in Pondicherry proposed to Her that such a township should be started. She gave her blessings. The concept was then put before the Govt. of India, who gave their backing and took it to the General Assembly of UNESCO. In 1966 UNESCO passed a unanimous resolution commending it as a project of importance to the future of humanity, thereby giving their full encouragement.

Why Auroville?

The purpose of Auroville is to realise human unity – in diversity. Today Auroville is recognised as the first and only internationally endorsed ongoing experiment in human unity and transformation of consciousness, also concerned with - and practically researching into - sustainable living and the future cultural, environmental, social and spiritual needs of mankind.

When did Auroville start?

On 28th February 1968 some 5,000 people assembled near the banyan tree at the centre of the future township for an inauguration ceremony attended by representatives of 124 nations, including all the states of India. The representatives brought with them some soil from their homeland, to be mixed in a white marble- clad, lotus-shaped urn, now sited at the focal point of the Amphitheatre. At the same time the Mother gave Auroville its 4-point Charter.

Source: http://www.auroville.org/

A volunteer led her to the accommodation she had booked. The self contained studio had an attached bathroom and a kitchen with a veranda and a patch of green in front. There were ceiling fans but no air conditioner. She felt belonged instantly.

Something told her that spectacular things awaited her though she was not sure if anything could change in her life now. What was left? "Me, me," the hazy form danced right in front of her wide open eyes, "Come to me. Be with me. I will never leave you. I am the only person who can give you peace and happiness." She shook her head vigorously in the hope to shake the tormentor off her mind too. It went away the next moment. She didn't know how but it did. At least that was a relief.

She felt her neck totally relaxed too. The catch she had developed while dragging her luggage from the conveyor belt at the airport had gone. She rotated her neck to make sure and realized it was back to normal. Wow, she had just stepped on this land and one nagging ache had taken its leave! Life was surely about to get better.

She checked into her studio, unpacked and got into the shower. As the hot water ran down her body, she felt waves of relaxation descend on her. Fifteen minutes later, she was dressed in casual linen pants teamed with a short cotton kurti, wore her flip flops, all set to head out to grab a bite somewhere. As she locked her room and turned back, she saw a couple of firangs smiling at her while continuing to walk. She smiled back and joined them. The man, Mark, was an architect by profession and his companion, Victoria, was a writer. Americans by birth they were in their mid 40s and visited Auroville every year for two months. According to them, the time they spent at Matrimandir rejuvenated them like nothing ever did or could. She had read about it in the brochures. They were anyway headed there now and they asked her to join them if she wished. She said she was hungry and they offered to take her to a place nearby where she could eat and then they could head to Matrimandir. She could do with some easy companionship and joined them.

The lunch was another near divine experience. They walked about a kilometer and entered into this thatched space where a spread of cool panna, fresh lime juices, sprouts, salads, rotis, rice, dal and curries was laid out. They chose a bench on which they placed their belongings and picked up a brass plate from the stack. They served whatever they wished to eat along with their choice of drinks in glasses and settled down on the bench. The food was wholesome, delicious and filling. Once they were done, she enquired about the bill and Mark told her that they could drop whatever they felt like in the dropbox at the exit. Menaka felt as if they had entered a different world and when she said it aloud, both of them commented that it was indeed far removed from the rest of the world. With their stomachs at ease, they started walking towards Matrimandir.

The Matrimandir was described in the literature she had read as a shrine of the Universal Mother and the Soul of Auroville. It was meant for those who, in the Mother's words, were sincere and serious and truly wanted to learn to concentrate. It was not a temple in the conventional sense of the word; it was neither a place of worship, nor associated with any religion, whether ancient, present, new or future.

They reached the Viewing Point, in the south of the Park of Unity, a raised garden area which provided visitors with a beautiful view of the Matrimandir and its surroundings. It looked spectacular. They collected their passes and trekked for a while to get to the Matrimandir. She had read earlier that Matrimandir was Mother's conception as "A place...for trying to find one's consciousness. It is like the Force, the central Force of Auroville, the cohesive Force of Auroville" in her own words.

Seemed like just what she was seeking. Victoria described one of her meditation experiences after several sessions as the ultimate revelation of her inner self. Menaka couldn't fathom the depth of it. Victoria explained, "Meditation is like washing a dirty cloth. Every session, a little dirt goes away like it happens in the first rinse. Just like how after several rinses, the original colour of the cloth returns, we need to keep at it till the mind becomes totally clean and aware. The trick is in not getting discouraged initially thinking that nothing has happened." Menaka responded saying she had never ever meditated in her life; her mind was always crowded with thoughts; and that's why she had enrolled for the workshop to get a hang of it.

As luck would have it, Victoria turned out to be the guru Menaka was supposed to train with. Menaka laughed out loud at the irony of an American guru teaching an Indian her own country's age old science. Mark remarked, "Mysterious ways of the universe." She couldn't agree more. Of all the people, the first one she had crossed paths with turned out to be the guru she was seeking. Mysterious, indeed!

They walked back to her studio and Victoria showed her, her cottage on the way in which the meditation classes would be conducted. She had to get there at 6 AM sharp everyday for 15 days. Menaka was quite eager to begin but she had to wait till the next day. The rest of the day, Menaka spent in the balcony reading Paulo Coelho's "Victoria decides to die." Later she noticed the coincidence in the title of the book and the name of the guru she had just met. Victoria and Mark believed that the universe spoke to us through symbols and coincidences. Whatever we came across or experienced, according to them, were not random occurrences. They were all meant to be for us to learn our lessons. "And also to understand me," the hazy form manifested seated right next to her. Strangely, this time she experienced no fear but she still couldn't see clearly even from such close quarters. Without intending anything in particular, she asked the hazy form, "Why don't you move that cloak off from your face? I want to see your face. Who are you?" The hazy form laughed that familiar muffled mocking laughter and said, "I am sitting so close to you. Why don't you make an effort and move it? The help you're looking for is at the end of your arm." Menaka looked at her hand in her lap, on the book she had just placed down when she had heard the voice next to her and understood the meaning. She raised her hand and turned to the side with the intention of doing what the hazy form suggested, but it wasn't there. There was nobody next to her. She had started seeing visions with her eyes open. The 'nightmares' were not as menacing either when they were nightmares. On the contrary, she felt she knew this person, the voice sounded very familiar, it was definitely somebody she had known in her past. Anyway, the good news was that Victoria had assured her she would understand the meaning of the messages this hazy form was trying to convey. She didn't have to wait for long.

Chapter XVIII

Several miles away, in a remote village in Telangana, Yadagiri was having a meal with his wife Rani and their daughters after a hard day's toil in the agricultural fields. As usual, this year too there was severe drought. But fortunately, they had found water where they had dug a well. They had left Hyderabad a day after their employer was found dead in his sleep and returned to their village in the remote Karimnagar district, known for extreme heat and poverty. Luckily, he and Rani had found jobs as farm hands in the nearby fields. Luckily again, the land owner had found water. They worked hard from the crack of dawn to sunset, planting seeds and drawing water from the well for irrigation. The only crop that grew in their area was turmeric which is least affected by pests and diseases. They were in the process of making uniform beds for planting turmeric in the entire 18 acres of land.

It was a long process. They had to get the land ready in the monsoon months. And then after the harvest, the rhizomes had to be boiled, dried and polished. But Yadagiri had no complaints. Life was extremely tough for his daughters. They had to trek eight kilometres everyday to reach the Government School in which they had been admitted. Back in Hyderabad, Menaka had ensured they went to good English medium schools. She even took care of their transport in addition to the fee. She was an angel. That's why he HAD to leave Hyderabad. He had to protect his family from the aftermath of saab's death just in case somebody suspected foul play. But there had been no foul play, he consoled himself. Just then he saw Rani at a distance walking towards him. The women worked on the other side of the fields. It was lunch time and they made it a point to eat lunch together. Rani packed jowar rotis with dry red chili chutney and sometimes daal, when they could afford, in an aluminium box which she carried with her to the field. She would wake up every morning, start cooking at 4, pack their kids' lunch boxes, theirs and they would set out together to the fields. She brought a smile to his face always, invariably, regardless of where they were. She was very unhappy to leave the city especially because she wanted their daughters to be educated so that their lives would be more dignified. She had protested when he pressurised her to pack up immediately after Dev saab's death. "How can we do this to Amma?" she had pleaded with him, "She needs us more now. And what about our daughters? Their schools will reopen soon." He had prevailed over her lying that they would return after a brief holiday. Once they reached there, he had quickly found jobs for both of them. She had asked him repeatedly why he was doing this. Sometimes angrily, sometimes beseechingly, sometimes she cried in the nights softly which he pretended to not hear. But there was nothing he could do. He was helpless. He was sure she would become normal as time passed. Time was the biggest healer. She came to him with the same sombre expression she always had ever since they had left Hyderabad. They settled down in their usual place after washing their hands and began to eat in silence. Her face was losing its softness with the harsh weather and work conditions here. His heart welled with affection and he stroked her cheek. She raised her eyes to look at him and tears trickled down her cheeks. "I am sorry Rani," he blurted out, "There is nothing I can do now." She swallowed her food and asked, "Why not? Why can't we go back? Amma will be happy to take us back. You know how much she loved all of us. I did everything you told me always without questioning. Didn't I? I even added sugar to the tea and lime juice saab drank and the sweets I cooked for him because you said Saab would become sweeter and behave better with everyone. But he died all of a sudden! And now she needs all of us even more." Yadagiri was startled when she brought up the subject suddenly. Did she have an inkling why he made her do that? He looked at her face and realized she had no clue. She was just talking random stuff. She continued, "Why are you not letting me call her at least. We told her we would be returning in a week. It's been more than a month now. I know you have no intentions of taking us back to Hyderabad. That's why you are sending the kids to the local school here." He sat their quietly without saying a word because he knew if he spoke he would blurt out everything. That Prabhat sir had told him to tell his wife to add sugar instead of substitutes to his beverages and desserts. And he is the one who had told him to leave the city a day after the funeral. Yadagiri knew he was an extra player in the grand scheme of Prabhat's plan.

One day he was working in the garden muttering under his breath after he had been abused by Dev sir because he (Yadagiri) had requested him (Dev) not to use expletives for amma. He sensed somebody's presence behind him. When he turned back, he saw Prabhat looking at him seriously. Presuming he had heard what he had muttered, Yadagiri had blurted out, "It's not right sir. Amma is an angel and Saab keeps illtreating her and cursing her behind her back. I couldn't tolerate it anymore. That's why I took him on today. And he asked me to shut up or get lost from here. I have served this house for so long, my wife is always at his beck and call, neglecting her health and our children and this is what we get in return." Prabhat had shushed him and said, "Quiet, quiet, he may hear you. Come outside and get into my car. We can talk somewhere else." And then he left closing the gate behind him. Yadagiri washed the mud off his hands, wiped them and went to his quarters behind the house, changed his shirt and walked out. When he stepped out, he saw Prabhat signalling him to get into the car. He got into the front seat and Prabhat drove. Prabhat spoke to him gently saying he wanted his help to make Dev a better person who respected everybody. All he had to do was to get his wife Rani to replace the sugar substitute with sugar in everything Dev drank or ate. "It will make him a sweet person. His words are very bitter because he lacks sweetness in him." Yadagiri agreed saying, "Anything saab. I just want him to treat amma well and stop cursing her and shouting at her. It's okay if he abuses us because our fates are like this only. Nobody respects us. Even in our village, our landlord used to make us beg for our wages and kick us sometimes. Saab, we come to cities so that we can earn better money to educate our kids and eat a belly full everyday. I am used to being beaten and abused saab but I feel terrible when Dev saab is so mean to Rani who is so sincere. Sometimes he doesn't even remember our names and addresses us like we are lowly animals." Prabhat heard him out patiently, handed a 1000 rupee note to him which he reluctantly accepted and said, "Just do what I tell you. Everything will be fine. Dev won't abuse or hurt anybody if you do what I tell you."

Yadagiri went along and narrated the 'sweet theory' to Rani who executed the plan without any ado. He hadn't given it much thought until Prabhat came to his quarters when Dev saab's body was lying in the living room and thrust an envelope in his hand and said, "Go back to your village tomorrow. I will call you soon and let you know when you can return. Just tell Menaka that there is an emergency in your village. And don't speak to me in front of people. In any case, I will be leaving shortly. Put your mobile off. Call me after a month. My number is on a piece of paper in the envelope." With that he turned back and walked into the house. Yadagiri didn't know what to make of it. He undid the staple pin and looked into the envelope. There was a wad of 1000 rupees, maybe a lakh of rupees in there. He had no choice but to put it in the cupboard and lock up. He was warned by Prabhat to not talk to him.

On the bus ride to their village, when most passengers had dozed off, he stayed awake letting the sequence of events sink in. He was missing something. He had probably played a role, unwittingly, in the sudden death of Dev saab. There was more to the 'sweet theory' than he realized. And if his suspicion was right, he was happy to be a part of the scheme which liberated his angel and many others who were at the receiving end of one man's tyranny.

He wondered how Menaka madam was coping. He remembered the envelope he had kept locked in his cupboard. It was time to call Prabhat sir.

Prabhat was at work when an unknown number flashed on his cell phone. Life had been uneventful since Dev's death. Nothing of consequence had happened. He hadn't met his sister since the funeral. She had called sometime back. His heart pounded away with an unknown fear when he answered the call but was relieved to know that she had called to inform him that she was going to be away for a while in Pondicherry. He had asked her to take care and keep in touch. Deep down he knew she was going to be fine. After all, he had done what he could to liberate her from all painful bondage. Moreover, the man had died of excess sweetness, his favourite taste! First he had made sure through Rani that Dev's sugar reached as high as it could get, then he had requested Dev's diabetologist Dr. Gupta (his 'special' friend) to advise him to discontinue insulin injections for a week ostensibly to try nature cure. That evening Prabhat had dropped in to see his sister knowing well that she was out and Dev had asked him if he would join him for a drink. Sure enough he had, well, that's how he had planned it all. After the second drink, when Dev complained of uneasiness, Prabhat had pretended to look into Dev's phone book and pretended to call Dr. Gupta and said he had advised him to take an increased dose of insulin than usual. From hyperglycaemia to hypoglycaemia, it happened in a flash while Prabhat just watched the man slip rapidly. He had somehow helped him reach the bed and made him lie there. Prabhat knew he would slip into a coma. But he hadn't expected that evening to be Dev's last.

He had just wanted to torture him and make him suffer for a bit. That's why when he got the news of Dev's death late that night, he was shell shocked. And then he panicked. What if his sister had seen him walk out while she walked into the compound that night? That's why he had convinced his unsuspecting partner in crime, Yadagiri to leave home with his family. But nothing had happened like he had feared. Menaka had called Dr. Gupta who took half an hour to reach their house in an ambulance but it was too late by then. He had pronounced that the death was due to cardiac arrest.

He answered the phone only to hear an unfamiliar coarse voice which turned out to be Yadagiri's. He smiled and told him he could get back to Menaka's home whenever he wanted. "Akka is away for some time. Why don't you call her and check when you could get back? But remember one thing, never ever tell her that I had dropped in that night. If you want your Amma to be happy for the rest of her life, you shouldn't remind her of anything related to that night. Don't let Rani speak about anything either. At last, akka has found peace. She has nobody other than you to look after her. Her peace is in your hands now," he said in a sad tone. Yadagiri bought the `peace theory' just like he had done with the `sweet theory' feeling genuinely responsible for Menaka's well being. When he told Rani to call amma, she was super thrilled. Their daughters overheard the conversation and began jumping with delight. They loved their life in the city and Menaka. They had never gone hungry thanks to huge left overs that were passed on to them every day. And they could go back to their school wearing neatly pressed uniforms. Without wasting time, Rani grinned as she switched on the phone that had been lying in the cupboard for more than a month.

It was the first day of the `Dhyan' workshop. Ten of them including Menaka had enrolled with Victoria to learn meditation. Nine of them had tried meditating earlier but hadn't made any progress. For Menaka, it was the first time, so she didn't know what to expect. She had read a few articles, seen TV programmes, but surprisingly it turned out very different. She had seen pictures of people sitting on the floor with crossed legs, eyes closed in deep concentration. Victoria's method was different. Actually, there was no method. All she asked them to do was to focus on the breath. Inhale shorter breaths and exhale longer breaths. Wasn't as simple as it sounded, though. To begin with, Menaka realized that her breathing was faulty. When she was asked to feel her breath, she noticed that her chest moved instead of her abdomen like Victoria was guiding them to do. She had to consciously focus her attention on abdominal breathing. She was just about beginning to get a hang of it when she heard Victoria's voice guiding them out of it. But one thing was certain. Not one thought had entered her mind. And that in itself was a huge achievement. A light breakfast of muesli, toast, butter, dry fruits and nuts was served which they ate as they got familiar with each other. It was an interesting experience for Menaka to meet so many different people. Suddenly she felt as if she had literally been a frog in the well. So caught up in her limited world that she had thought it was the whole world. Even when she was working, the kind of people she met were predictable. Here each one had a different background and therefore different stories to tell. After the breakfast, Mark took them through different forms of meditation and natural healing. In addition to the physical health he also spoke about emotional health and concluded that there were 6 dimensions of wellness:

Physical – Caring for one's health
Emotional – Managing & Expressing feelings
Spiritual – Appreciating life, Having values
Social – Having positive relationships
Intellectual – Acquiring knowledge & skills
Vocational – Finding fulfillment through work and volunteerism

"We can attain higher levels of wellness and experience fulfillment only if we pay attention to all the aspects. Health did not mean just physical. It was the state of the entire being, the integration of body, mind and spirit and its ongoing pursuit of a healthy balanced lifestyle," he concluded.

This was quite a revelation for Menaka. She was shocked when she learnt that she just exercised and ate the right foods; she had focused only one dimension of wellness so far. She was unhealthy and ill by these standards. She and most people she knew had no idea how to manage and express feelings, had no appreciation for life, not many had positive relationships, nobody actively acquired knowledge or any new skills, some may have been involved with their work but fulfillment? She wasn't so sure. Voluntary work for the benefit of others? Nah, not one soul she knew did any of these! No wonder they felt so empty from within. Wow, life!

The following days were focused on every single aspect of the six dimensions of wellness. A detailed self analysis was the main component of the programme. Once they became more aware of themselves through the questions they answered, specific exercises were designed for them to do in solitude. These included affirmations, conscious awareness of every word and action, staying in the body, being mindful of every moment and movement. Easier said than understood.

As she went through each day, a new layer was being revealed. While her concentration on breath got more and more focused, her inner being was peeling off layers and layers of self defeating thought processes and belief systems. She was shocked when she learnt so many self sabotaging beliefs she had about herself. She was even more shocked to realize that she had an unfailing knack for self fulfilling prophecies.

She recognized that her failure in retaining the purity of the relationship she shared with Rishi was mainly because she didn't believe he genuinely loved her. Somehow, she always felt that she would lose him. Underlying this fact was her own belief that she didn't deserve to be loved. Yes, that was the truth!

She didn't know if Rishi contributed to her fears. But the fact was that her inability to believe that she deserved to be loved coupled with her fear of losing him, resulted in her losing him even though she was the one who had opted out.

It was also probably why she never trusted Dev's devotion for her. She only saw what she wanted to see. She held beliefs that fed her fears.

Chapter XIX

A fortnight went by quickly, probably the quickest that time had passed in her life so far, with her getting better with meditation. She was able to now sit for a good 20 minutes without her focus shifting from her breath. That thoughtless state was pure bliss. Being mindless for a brief while made her mindful for the rest of the day. She felt energized, her concentration had grown manifold and she felt light as if a burden had lifted off her shoulders and chest. For no particular reason she would feel happy. Every sunrise, every sunset, each time she saw the moon or heard the birds' chirrup, the sight of a flower in full bloom, dew drops on leaves, butterflies in the air, she felt elated as if she was connected to every instance of nature. She felt more empathy for people around her.

On the last evening of the workshop, everybody spoke of their experience, their learning and how it had changed them. Victoria and Mark had organized dinner for all the participants at the end of the workshop. Most of them had planned to visit the Matrimandir the next day to meditate.

That night, just as she was dozing off, the hazy form appeared in a flash but this time she could see the outline of the figure rather clearly. It definitely was a woman. But the face was still hazy though she thought she saw a smile. Good, at least the terrorizing quality of the visions had disappeared. She could deal with them now.

The next morning she woke up at 4 AM even though she didn't have to reach anywhere. In just a fortnight her sleep cycle had changed from what it had been for 25 years. There was no habit that a human being couldn't change if they want to. She had also learnt in the workshop that it took 28 days to replace an old habit with a new practice. Obviously, there was truth in it. For years she had been a late riser but all it had taken was a fortnight of new practice.

After a leisurely breakfast she had prepared for herself, she got ready and left her studio around 11.30 for Matrimandir. She aimed to get in by noon after which it was supposed to be magical inside when the rays of the sun entered the meditation hall.

Matrimandir's history was fascinating even to read:

Towards the end of 1965 the Mother decided that a lone Banyan tree would be the geographical centre of the future town. At the time the site was almost totally barren.

Early 1968, the Mother gave their names to Matrimandir's twelve Gardens:

> *Existence, Consciousness, Bliss, Light, Life, Power, Wealth, Utility, Progress, Youth, Harmony, Perfection.*

On 28th February 1968, Auroville's inauguration ceremony took place around a white Urn, shaped like a lotus bud, which now stands at the focus of a large amphitheatre. Youth representing each state of India and each country of the world placed a handful of soil of their respective state/country in this Urn while a welcoming message and Auroville's Charter were read in various Indian and foreign languages.

Late 1969, the Mother explained to an American horticulturist, Narad, whom she had called to start the Matrimandir Gardens: '*It must be a thing of great beauty, of such beauty that when people come they will say "Ah, this is it". It must be an expression of that consciousness which we are trying to bring down*'. She added: '*One must know how to move from consciousness to consciousness*'.

In January 1970, the Mother asked a French architect, Roger Anger, to start working on Matrimandir – saying that she had had repeated visions of its Inner Chamber and gave him a measured drawing of it, which an Ashram engineer, Udar, had drawn according to her instructions. She said that she had not 'seen' the rest of the building.

In March 1970, Roger Anger presented to the Mother a model of the Inner Chamber along with five different models for the Matrimandir. She selected one of these models, a slightly flattened golden sphere, and the architect worked further on it.

In 1970, in answer to repeated questions from an Ashram artist, Huta, the Mother dictated to her son, André, this reply: *"It has been decided and remains decided that the Matrimandir will be surrounded with water. However, water is not available just now and will be available only later; so it is decided to build the Matrimandir now and surround it with water only later; perhaps in a few years' time... The Matrimandir will be built now and water brought round it later."* The Lake's size and shape were however not finalised during the Mother's lifetime.

In February 1971, the Mother approved a new model presented to her by Roger Anger. It represented Matrimandir on an oval island. The Mandir looked like a lotus in full bloom emerging from twelve large 'petals'. This model defined the layout and contouring of this island with its twelve gardens, the banyan tree, the Amphitheatre, etc. This model depicts the Matrimandir Island as having the same oval shape as Matrimandir's vertical section but ten times larger (360m x 290m).

On 21st February 1971, Matrimandir's foundation stone was laid. Three weeks later, on 14th March, excavation work started. At first only Aurovilians dug, but the excavation was so large that some 400 local labourers had to be hired to dig it faster.

Early 1971, a Nursery was established in Matrimandir's vicinity to acclimate, study and propagate the plants required for the gardens. When the Mother was asked whether the people working at Matrimandir Nursery should stop working there and help dig the huge hole required for its foundations, she replied: *"No, the gardens are as important as the Matrimandir itself."*

On 21st February 1972, the first concreting (of the foundation) took place.

In one of her messages, the Mother wrote: '*The Matrimandir wants to be the symbol of the Universal Mother according to Sri Aurobindo's teaching*'; and early 1972, she named Matrimandir's North, South, East and West pillars after the four '*Aspects*' or '*Personalities*' of the Supreme Mother, that is respectively: *Mahakali, Maheshwari, Mahalakshmi, Mahasaraswati;* and the twelve meditation rooms, which are located inside Matrimandir's twelve large 'petals', after her twelve '*Virtues*' or '*Qualities*':

Sincerity, Humility, Gratitude, Perseverance, Aspiration, Receptivity, Progress, Courage, Goodness, Generosity, Equality, Peace.

On 17th November 1973, the concreting of the four concrete pillars which support Matrimandir ended. Exactly at the same time the Mother left her body.

*The Matrimandir wants to be
the symbol of the Universal Mother
according to Sri Aurobindo's teaching.*

*

Matrimandir is dedicated to the *Universal Mother*, a Presence or Being that has been experienced and worshiped, under different names, in most cultures of the world since time immemorial. The ancient Egyptians named her 'Isis', the Incas '*Pachamama*', the Japanese '*Kwannon*', the Hindus '*Aditi*', the Catholics identified her with '*Virgin Mary*', etc.

Matrimandir isn't dedicated to any particular emanation or incarnation of the Mother. Sri Aurobindo explains below the difference he makes between the "*universal*" or "*cosmic*" Mother and the "*individual*" Mothers.

* * *

"... *it will be the 'Pavilion of the Mother'; but not this* [the Mother points to herself]: *the Mother, the true Mother, the principle of the Mother. (I say 'Mother'*

*because Sri Aurobindo used the word, otherwise I would have put something else –
I would have put 'creative principle' or 'realising principle' or... something of that
sort.)"*

(The Mother, Mother's Agenda, 23.06.65)

* * *

*If the same being appeared simultaneously in a group where there were Christians,
Buddhists, Hindus, Shintoists, it would be named by absolutely different names.
Each would say, in reference to the appearance of the being, that he was like this
or like that, all differing and yet it would be one and the same manifestation. You
have the vision of one in India whom you call the Divine Mother, the Catholics
say it is the Virgin Mary, and the Japanese call it Kwannon, the Goddess of Mercy,
and others would give other names. It is the same Force, the same Power, but the
images made of it are different in different faiths.*

(The Mother, Questions and Answers 1929-1931, Page: 18)

* * *

*The One whom we adore as the Mother is the divine Conscious Force that dominates
all existence, one and yet so many-sided that to follow her movement is impossible
even for the quickest mind and for the freest and most vast intelligence. The Mother
is the consciousness and force of the Supreme and far above all she creates. But
something of her ways can be seen and felt through her embodiments and the more
seizable because more defined and limited temperament and action of the goddess
forms in whom she consents to be manifest to her creatures.*

*There are three ways of being of the Mother of which you can become aware when
you enter into touch of oneness with the Conscious Force that upholds us and the
universe. Transcendent, the original supreme Shakti, she stands above the worlds
and links the creation to the ever unmanifest mystery of the Supreme. Universal,
the cosmic Mahashakti, she creates all these beings and contains and enters, supports
and conducts all these million processes and forces. Individual, she embodies the
power of these two vaster ways of her existence, makes them living and near to us
and mediates between the human personality and the divine Nature.*

The one original transcendent Shakti, the Mother stands above all the worlds and bears in her eternal consciousness the Supreme Divine. Alone, she harbours the absolute Power and the ineffable Presence; containing or calling the Truths that have to be manifested, she brings them down from the Mystery in which they were hidden into the light of her infinite consciousness and gives them a form of force in her omnipotent power and her boundless life and a body in the universe. The Supreme is manifest in her for ever as the everlasting Sachchidananda, manifested through her in the worlds as the one and dual consciousness of Ishwara-Shakti and the dual principle of Purusha-Prakriti, embodied by her in the Worlds and the Planes and the Gods and their Energies and figured because of her as all that is in the known worlds and in unknown others. All is her play with the Supreme; all is her manifestation of the mysteries of the Eternal, the miracles of the Infinite. All is she, for all are parcel and portion of the divine Conscious-Force. Nothing can be here or elsewhere but what she decides and the Supreme sanctions; nothing can take shape except what she moved by the Supreme perceives and forms after casting it into seed in her creating Ananda.

The Mahashakti, the universal Mother, works out whatever is transmitted by her transcendent consciousness from the Supreme and enters into the worlds that she has made; her presence fills and supports them with the divine spirit and the divine all-sustaining force and delight without which they could not exist. That which we call Nature or Prakriti is only her most outward executive aspect; she marshals and arranges the harmony of her forces and processes, impels the operations of Nature and moves among them secret or manifest in all that can be seen or experienced or put into motion of life. Each of the worlds is nothing but one play of the Mahashakti of that system of worlds or universe, who is there as the cosmic Soul and Personality of the transcendent Mother. Each is something that she has seen in her vision, gathered into her heart of beauty and power and created in her Ananda.

But there are many planes of her creation, many steps of the Divine Shakti. At the summit of this manifestation of which we are a part there are worlds of infinite existence, consciousness, force and bliss over which the Mother stands as the unveiled eternal Power. All beings there live and move in an ineffable completeness and unalterable oneness, because she carries them safe in her arms forever. Nearer to us are the worlds of a perfect supramental creation in which the Mother is the supramental Mahashakti, a Power of divine omniscient Will and omnipotent Knowledge always apparent in its unfailing works and spontaneously perfect in every process. There all movements are the steps of the Truth; there all beings are souls and powers and bodies of the divine Light; there all experiences are seas and floods and waves of an intense and absolute Ananda. But here where we dwell are the worlds of the Ignorance, worlds of mind and life and body separated in consciousness from their source, of which this earth is a significant centre and its evolution a crucial process. This too with all its obscurity and struggle and imperfection is upheld by the Universal Mother; this too is impelled and guided to its secret aim by the Mahashakti.

The Mother as the Mahashakti of this triple world of the Ignorance stands in an intermediate plane between the supramental Light, the Truth life, the Truth creation which has to be brought down here and this mounting and descending hierarchy of planes of consciousness that like a double ladder lapse into the nescience of Matter and climb back again through the flowering of life and soul and mind into the infinity of the Spirit. Determining all that shall be in this universe and in the terrestrial evolution by what she sees and feels and pours from her, she stands there above the Gods and all her Powers and Personalities are put out in front of her for the action and she sends down emanations of them into these lower worlds to intervene, to govern, to battle and conquer, to lead and turn their cycles, to direct the total and the individual lines of their forces. These Emanations are the many divine forms and personalities in which men have worshipped her under different names throughout the ages. But also she prepares and shapes through these Powers and their emanations the minds and bodies of her Vibhutis, even as she prepares and shapes minds and bodies for the Vibhutis of the Ishwara, that she may manifest in the physical world and in the disguise of the human consciousness some ray of her power and quality and presence. All the scenes of the earthplay have been like a drama arranged and planned and staged by her with the cosmic Gods for her assistants and herself as a veiled actor.

(Sri Aurobindo, '*The Mother*')

* * *

As she walked along, she spotted the golden dome which glittered in the bright sunlight. The sight was mesmerizing. She walked in with a group of people greeting them with a smile, some of whom she knew from the meditation class. They were asked to leave their footwear and get into soft velvety white flip flops. Everything inside the amphitheatre was pristine white. They walked through the tunnel-like corridor and entered the inner chamber which was built according to repeated visions of the mother. Right in the centre of the hall was an oval crystal globe directly under the aperture in the centre of

Matrimandir's rooftop. A single ray of the sun was projected by a mirror down on the crystal placed exactly in the centre. The heliostat controlled by a computer programme, which moved the mirror across the sun's path throughout the day, made this happen.

This mirror projected sunlight into a lens that in turn projected the single sun ray down on the crystal. To make sure that the ray strikes the crystal exactly in the centre, a photo sensor was installed in the path of the ray itself and relayed the data on the ray's position to the computer, which in turn adjusted the ray to the correct position if necessary. The result was a spectacular dazzle when the sun ray hit the top of the crystal and passed through the centre.

There were 12 meditation rooms in the shape of flattened spheres. The inside walls of each room were in a different colour. Sincerity was pale Blue. Humility and Gratitude were in different shades of Green. Perseverance was yellow. Receptivity was Orange. Courage was in Red. Generosity in Violet. Peace in dark Blue. All the other rooms had colours in between these.

One had to choose a particular virtue and sit there to concentrate while being bathed in the light of the corresponding colour. One had to sit on a concrete slab of white marble which seemed to float inside the flattened sphere. The rooms were air-conditioned and there was an object of concentration at eye level if you sat on the floor. The object was translucent oval made of glass which was placed in front of a small window through which natural light entered at day time and at night, electrical light produced the same effect. An Auroville architect had designed some geometrical patterns on these objects of concentration, a different pattern for each room.

A circular corridor gave access to these 12 meditation rooms. The outer wall of each of these sections of the corridor had red sand stones.

Menaka was spellbound as she took in the surroundings. She contemplated for a bit and chose the room for Receptivity. She wanted to receive information about the hazy form that she had visions of. She made herself comfortable on the floor, took a few deep breaths with closed eyes, opened them to focus on the object of concentration. She lost track of time as she got drawn into a trance. And that's when it happened. Out of the blue, the object of concentration disappeared and in its place was the hazy form. She had already noticed during her last vision that it was a female figure. Now she could see the colour of the dress clearly. She was wearing a purple kurti on white pants and seated cross legged. As Menaka focused on the face, slowly the hood disappeared and she noticed the waist length thick brown hair falling in waves. And then, one by one beginning from the forehead, each feature started appearing clearly. Almond eyes, small nose, full lips and a pronounced chin. The entire form, face, body, everything was unmistakably. Menaka was astounded at what she saw. It was her own reflection. Even the clothes she wore were exactly what she was wearing right now. Her reflection laughed the same muffled mocking laughter and uttered, "Do you recognize me now? I am you. I was just speaking aloud what you were feeling deep within. I was voicing your fears. The fears that drove your actions." Menaka found her voice somehow and asked, "Why did you scare me then? Why did you warn me against Rishi? Why did you ask me to leave him and say that I would die if I didn't?" Her inner voice replied gently, "That was your innermost fear. That he was non-existent for you. You felt everything you said went unheard. You felt he didn't notice you. You were feeling suffocated. You felt you were dying each day." Menaka wasn't convinced yet. "What about the time you asked me to go to Dev whom I had just met? Why was I wearing torn clothes and why did I have wounds on my body?" she asked. "You felt very insecure with Rishi. You were scared you will be torn to bits and your self-respect was wounded because you felt you continued to live with him even when he made fun of your agonies. And you felt he just didn't care about how you looked outside or felt inside." Menaka couldn't stop herself from crying. Tears rolled down her cheeks as she continued asking, "What about the dream in which my upper part and lower part were pulled in the opposite directions? And all that blood in between?" Her reflection laughed again softly, mockingly. "Oh Menaka, Menaka, can't you see it now, at least? You were being torn in two directions by Rishi and Dev. Your upper part in which your heart and mind are were being pulled away by Rishi while the lower part with your legs and feet was being dragged by Dev. You felt deep pain and restless thoughts because of Rishi. You felt your movements were being restricted by Dev. Dreams are the language of your subconscious. Their only purpose is to help you to get in touch with your inner self. Even while I was trying to talk to you, conveying your fears to you, you kept running away from me, which means you were running away from yourself. Did you notice in the last few days, after you started discovering yourself, I even sat next to you once and you didn't get scared. And you even noticed my smile. You know why?" her reflection asked. Menaka replied, "Yes, I do now. I had begun to get in touch with my true self. I had begun to overcome my fears, I had begun to accept myself the way I am, I had begun to make peace with my inner demons, I had begun to like myself." "Bingo, there you are! Now that you know yourself, know that you can be your best friend or worst enemy. Everything is within you. You are the only person who can make you happy. Look at you. You're so happy for the first time in your own company. Earlier, when you were seeking happiness through the presence or absence of others, you were so miserable, so unhappy, so restless. You deserve to be happy Menaka. That is your only purpose in this world," saying this her refeflection walked towards her and hugged her. She felt utmost comfort. She felt secure and elated like never before. In the mirror that was in front of her, she looked at her image. It was whole. It was one. Her form and she had merged into one complete being.

Epilogue

One letter changes a word. One word, a sentence and one sentence a paragraph. One paragraph, an entire story.

Look what happened to mine!

"I didn't know what life meant until I realized, it's all about lo<u>v</u>ing a man. I could have created the life I dreamt of. But all I did was to keep wa<u>n</u>ting it."

"I didn't know what life meant until I realized, it's all about lo<u>s</u>ing a man. I could have created the life I dreamt of. But all I did was to keep wa<u>s</u>ting it."

From 'loving' to 'losing', 'wanting' to 'wasting', everything was my own creation.

Luckily for me, just when I thought I had 'nowhere' to go, I realized before it was too late that everything is 'now here.' I didn't have to go anywhere. It's all right here, right within.

Just a bit of reshuffling is all we need to do whenever we feel lost.